"Her toes did

"What did yo   loser to me.

"They kissed," I said, "but Stacy's toes didn't curl."

"Usually when two people kiss, they do it with their lips."

I ignored the sarcasm. "Our grandfather told us that our grandmother knew he was the right one for her because when they smooched, her toes curled."

"I see. What did *your* toes do when you and your artist guy kissed?"

His question caught me off guard. "Um . . . does it matter?"

"Yes," he said, "as evidence for your genetic theory."

That's not how I wanted it to matter. "Maybe it's not a genetic thing," I told him. "Did Kelly mention her toes after you kissed her?"

"No," he replied, "no, she didn't say a word."

Then we both turned back to the romantic little scene in front of us. I would've done anything to have been in Kelly's shoes the other night and to be in them tomorrow too—anything, of course, but tell Adam that.

ELIZABETH CHANDLER

BANTAM BOOKS
NEW YORK · TORONTO · LONDON · SYDNEY · AUCKLAND

RL 6, age 12 and up

I DO
A Bantam Book / March 1999

Cover photography by Michael Segal.

Produced by 17th Street Productions,
a division of Daniel Weiss Associates, Inc.
33 West 17th Street, New York, NY 10011.

ISBN: 0-553-49275-6

Published simultaneously in the United States and Canada

Bantam Books are published by Bantam Books, a division of Random
House, Inc. Its trademark, consisting of the words "Bantam Books" and
the portrayal of a rooster, is Registered in U.S. Patent and Trademark
Office and in other countries. Marca Registrada. Bantam Books, 1540
Broadway, New York, New York 10036.

PRINTED IN THE UNITED STATES OF AMERICA

OPM   0 9 8 7 6 5 4 3 2

To B. D. We did. 10/10/98

ONE

"ANY MESSAGES FOR me?" I asked as I entered the office for *The Pipeline,* our school newspaper.

"None in your box," replied Angela, our managing editor. "We've already given the police all the small, ticking packages and kidnapping threats."

I smiled and shrugged. "Another day, another unhappy jock." It wasn't my problem that some of Tilson High's athletes couldn't take criticism. And at that moment I wasn't very popular with the men's lacrosse team—especially their star, Adam Logan, and Adam's many fans.

"I have trouble imagining Adam Logan wanting to *kidnap* Jane," Kelly remarked. "Kidnappers and their victims have to spend time together." Then she turned and touched me lightly on the arm. Kelly was one of Adam's biggest fans and editor of our People page. She'd also stopped by after dismissal to

1

check her mailbox. She fished out a wad of gossipy notes from her "sources." "Just teasing, Jane."

"Yeah, yeah," I said.

Tom, our editor in chief, laughed. "Well, I'm sure our budget will cover the ransom," he said. "After a few hours of being grilled by Jane's questions, Adam wouldn't demand much money. He'd probably pay us to take her back."

I grimaced, and he laughed. Tom was a senior, a year older than I—a tall African American guy who both Angela and I'd had terrible crushes on freshman year. Now Angela had something worse than a crush. She was best buddies with him and, being second in command at the paper, the girl he was most likely to lean on, but she also wanted to be the girl he kissed. Tom had more sophisticated tastes, however, and was dating a college girl. That was just as well for me. I needed him as a sounding board and levelheaded editor in chief much more than I needed a romantic interest.

Actually, all of us depended on Tom. Our adviser, a reporter for *The Baltimore Sun,* taught journalism the first semester of every school year, then worked as an off-campus adviser second semester—very off campus. Tom stayed in contact with her, but he carried most of the responsibility for our four-page tabloid. It was a lot of work producing a weekly paper, especially for a school with eleven hundred students, but the juniors and seniors who wrote regular columns and did the editing were given independent class time to work and received full course credit.

"Just remember," I said, "if it wasn't for me, we

wouldn't have nearly as many letters to the editor."

"I'm grateful," Tom replied. "Adam's letter ran so long this week, I only had to write one paragraph for an editorial."

"Too bad Logan doesn't spend his time practicing shots in front of a goal instead of on a keyboard," I remarked. "He's got an incredible amount of ability. If he played up to it, I wouldn't get on him." I wheeled my desk chair over to the stack of newspapers that had been released that day. "I guess I should look at what he has to say."

"You mean you haven't read it yet?" Kelly asked, her blue eyes big with surprise. She was always checking the mailbox for letters to the editor to see if people had said anything about her.

"I didn't want his comments to influence what I wrote this week," I explained.

"And obviously they didn't," Tom said. "We've got another Jane Hardy analysis, calling it like she sees it."

Angela opened a copy of the paper that was sitting on top of her monitor and began reading from my column. "'If you're going to play a run-'em–gun-'em style of game, you had better make sure you've got some bullets—'"

"And we don't," she and I said at the same time.

"We really don't," I said, spinning around in my chair, then pushing off from the wall so that I ended up side by side with her. "We're not using our talent. Even our wins have made us look bad. In the first four games this season some of our shots at the goal have been—"

"'Like Ping-Pong balls lobbed at a goldfish bowl,'" Tom recalled from last week's column.

"And our passing game," I went on, determined to explain why the guys' lacrosse team made me crazy—

"'Is like a game of keep away among our own players,'" Angela remembered.

"So I like to write in images! It's how I reach my reader."

"Well, you reached the guys' lacrosse team," Angela replied, grinning.

"Instead of writing a letter, I wish they'd prove me wrong with a solid win," I said, then opened my copy of the paper to the op-ed page. "Well, let's see what Logan has to say."

Dear Editor,
    As captain of the varsity lacrosse team, I am writing to protest the poor coverage we have been receiving from your sports editor, Jane Hardy. Each week, instead of writing a clear and unbiased account of our games, she gabs on like a late-night talk-show host.

"Oh, really," I said. "'Like an obnoxious comedian, she oversimplifies the games so she can make jokes at the team's expense.'"

"Sounds like he got his feelings hurt," I muttered.

"'I don't mind her negative comments about my leadership skills.'" I glanced up from the paper for a moment and said, "Like heck you don't." Then I continued to read. "'But I resent the constant and unfair criticism of my teammates.'

"Okay, tell me how it's unfair," I commented.

"He does," Angela replied, "for the next two and a half columns. To be honest, I had no idea jocks could write that much."

I skimmed the letter. "Well, if he wants to convince me, he's going to have to give specific reasons and support them with stats and examples," I said. "All he does here is turn my own statements back on me, using things I've said to take clever shots at me—talk about sounding like a late-night talk-show host!"

But what really annoyed me were statements like, "Knowing the game of girls' lacrosse doesn't prepare a writer for guys' lacrosse." I read it aloud. "What's he implying by that?" I exclaimed.

"'If Hardy is truly interested in producing fair and informative articles rather than showing off as a writer . . .' yeah, yeah, yeah." I read on silently.

"I think you and Adam need to get together and talk things through," Kelly said.

I glanced up at her. "Why?"

"To make things friendlier between the team and the paper."

"Why would I want to do that?" I asked. Tom snorted.

"Because we're a *school* paper," Kelly replied, her face puckering with earnestness. "We're not *real* journalists, Jane. We're only supposed to tell everyone about the good things we're doing at Tilson High."

"That would make us a public-relations office."

She shrugged. "All I know is that there are a lot of people who like my columns."

"Like your feature about the nasty cafeteria lady who snarls if she has to give change? The woman you described as 'serious in her work and focused on efficiency'?"

"She's mailing the article to her grandchildren."

"I bet she is." I shook my head. "I hope they recognize her."

But the fact was, I knew there were students who loved Kelly's articles. To me the writing was dishonest, but this didn't bother some people—especially when she said something nice about them the following week.

I glanced at Tom, who was turning a pencil over and over in his hands. "What are you thinking?" I asked.

"Just thinking," he said.

"If you believe we need to smooth things over, you can have Kelly do a feature on Logan in the People section," I suggested, trying to draw Tom out, hoping he'd say, *Heck, no.* But he just nodded thoughtfully.

"*Could* I do a piece on him, Tom?" Kelly asked. "I think a lot of kids would be really interested."

Like the girls Kelly hangs around with, I thought.

"He's a terrific player—"

Could be, I added silently.

"—and has a great body and a great smile," she went on. "He's interesting—kind of the silent, mysterious type who studies a lot."

"Studying makes someone mysterious?" I asked, and Angela laughed.

I knew that Adam was really smart. We'd had one class together—sophomore English. He wouldn't say a word for a week, then we'd discuss a short story and he'd argue his view against anyone—including the teacher—and be totally persuasive. But that's as much contact as we'd had. Since I'd covered baseball sophomore year and those games often conflicted with lacrosse, I hadn't seen him play regularly until this year.

"I'll think about it, and we can run it by the rest of the staff next meeting," Tom said.

I stuffed an extra copy of the newspaper in my backpack.

"Heading off for the girls' game?" Angela asked me.

"Yup. I told Vinny, Sam, and Ellen that I wanted them on the fields and tennis court as soon as the players are. I can't be lagging behind."

Sam and Ellen were sophomores and already solid reporters. Vinny, an eager freshman and my trainee, was another story. He helped me cover the girls' lacrosse team, whose games were usually on Monday and Thursday, and the guys, who generally played Tuesday and Friday. If I could've cloned myself, I would've covered every sport—reporting on sports was what I lived to do.

I pushed hard against the school door, eager to get out into the sunlight. But the door gave way faster than I expected—someone was pulling it from the other side. I started to pitch headlong, then caught myself just in front of the person coming in. Adam Logan.

He was wearing a tattered practice shirt and was carrying an empty water bottle. He stared down at me with intense green eyes, his grip tightening on the bottle. Maybe he thought I'd look away, but I didn't. Then we silently continued on our separate ways, letting the metal door slam between us.

TWO

"**D**AISY JANE," MY grandfather greeted me when I arrived home from school that day.

When I was in first grade, back when I went to a different school in a different neighborhood, I didn't like my name. I thought it was boring. Plain Jane. I'm not bad looking, but I was never a pretty little girl who people noticed, like my cousin, Stacy. I have gray eyes and my mother's straight dark hair, which I wore shoulder length. Anyway, I'd thought the name Daisy was beautiful—it was a flower and sounded kind of like Stacy. So what had begun as an affectionate joke among members of my family had stuck as a pet name. But I would've died if anyone other than my best friend, Marnie, had known about it.

"Back from the thrill of victory and the agony of defeat," said Grandpa. "How'd the girls lacrosse team do?"

"We won," I replied, hanging my bike helmet

9

on the kitchen doorknob, then dropping my backpack on a chair. "Marnie played great."

"Glad to hear it." He lifted the lid off a pot simmering with fresh vegetable soup. "Did you bring my newspaper?"

"Yup. You get to read about me this week."

"Really!"

"Three columns," I told him. "Not exactly fan mail."

He laughed and removed a loaf of hot bread from the oven. "Good. I'll put it in the scrapbook I'm keeping for you."

My mother and I had lived with Grandpa for the last three years in a row house just beyond the Baltimore city line. It's a homey neighborhood, the one in which Mom grew up, with clusters of brick houses, row after row of steep slate roofs, covered porches, and big old trees. During my parents' rocky marriage, I'd spent a lot of time here and at my cousin Stacy's house. Here was where I was happiest.

After years of fighting, my father had finally left Mom and me, taking all our money with him. The two of us had struggled on our own for a while, but it was difficult. After all, my mother had dropped out of college when she'd been only halfway finished, giving up her dreams of an education and a career in order to marry my father. So when he left us, she suddenly had to find a way to make a decent enough living to support us.

Part of our solution was to move in permanently with Grandpa. Mom worked a secretarial job while taking night courses to finish her college degree. And Grandpa, who'd retired about a year ago, now played "mother" to both her and me.

Tuesday and Thursday nights were Mom's class nights, and I noticed that the shuttered door was closed between the kitchen and dining room. "Is she studying?" I asked Grandpa.

He nodded. "Another test from that maniac business prof."

I quietly opened the door and stuck my head into the dining room. Mom was sitting at the table, bent over a textbook, gripping her highlighter. She glanced up at me, her straight black hair tumbling into her eyes.

"How's it going, Mom?"

"Hi, Daisy. All right," she replied. "Good day?"

"Yeah. An interesting one," I said, then closed the door again to let her finish up. "Marnie got two goals and two assists," I told Grandpa as I unzipped my pack and pulled out his copy of *The Pipeline*. "I'm trying to convince her to cut her hair and play Tuesdays and Fridays for the guys' team," I added, spreading the paper on the bar built against one wall of our kitchen.

Grandpa peered over my shoulder. "Adam Logan," he read. "Isn't he that midfielder you're always talking about? The one you think is loaded with talent and not playing up to it?"

I nodded. "There are times when he plays like a middie for Johns Hopkins, but he's inconsistent. The team needs him to get his act together and set them on the right track."

11

"Well, those boys had a rough time with the head coach last year, the one the school fired," Grandpa recalled. "Sometimes it takes a while to recover from mismanagement and adjust to someone new."

"Coach Gryczgowski needs to light a fire under them."

Grandpa started reading the letter and smiled. "Looks to me like you did it for him." He read on, then laughed out loud. "This Logan fellow can write!"

"You don't have to admire him, Grandpa."

"Sure, I do. He can cradle and shoot, and turn a good phrase."

I grimaced just as my mother pulled back the shutter door and entered the kitchen.

"Is something wrong?" she asked.

"Your daughter's stirring up trouble again," Grandpa told her.

She glanced at what he was reading. "My daughter? Do you mean Jimmy Olsten, Junior?"

My grandfather's name is James Olstenheimer, but he wrote under Jimmy Olsten for the sports section of *The Baltimore Sun*.

"Don't tell me she's written something that other people don't agree with," Mom added with mock disbelief. "I've never known anyone in our family to do something like that."

Grandpa gave me a sly look. "The difference is, I was always right."

"Oh, please!" I said.

My mother smiled and helped herself to the soup. "Before I forget, Daisy—Stacy called. She wants to stop by and talk about the wedding."

"Well, that's a new topic," I replied. Since my cousin's engagement, she'd been talking about her wedding nonstop. The big event was to happen on the first of May, a little more than three weeks away, but I felt as if I'd already attended it numerous times. I'd been trying to seem really interested to make up for the fact that I'd declined her invitation to be a bridesmaid. I knew to be asked was an honor, but I just wasn't the type to hold a bouquet and wobble down a long aisle on silk-toed high heels, smiling at three-hundred and twenty-five guests.

"Stacy said there's some kind of problem," my mother added, frowning a little, spooning soup into a bowl.

Stacy's marriage worried Mom. Twenty-one did seem really young to settle down. I saw what had happened to my mother and would never, ever give up what I wanted to do for some guy. And I was determined not to put myself in a situation in which I was dependent on another person. But Stacy had finished college one semester early and could get a teaching job if her husband left her. And unlike my mother, Stacy's biggest dream had always been to get married. A large, pretty house, several kids, and a last name shorter than Olstenheimer—that was Stacy's greatest fantasy—all of which would be possible with her fiancé, a successful lawyer named Travis Avery Clarke III.

"Stacy said she'll come by as soon as she's finished at the hairdresser," my mother told me.

"She's trying *another* style?"

"Travis didn't like the last one," Mom replied.

"Or the one before that," I said.

"I know." Mom sighed, then glanced at the clock and gulped down the rest of her soup. Grandpa cut a thick slice of bread from the end of the warm loaf and wrapped it in plastic for her. "Got to run," Mom told us, then hurried off to gather her books and purse.

After she left for class, I set the kitchen bar for dinner. Grandpa and I had just sat down when the doorbell rang.

"I'll put out a third place," he said as I went to answer it.

Stacy came in, smelling like an entire salon. "Your hair looks pretty," I told her.

"You mean it?"

"You know I always say what I mean. It looks great, Stacy. But I liked the last style too. Actually, they look a lot alike."

"It's different," she said quickly. "See? This part around the ear."

I studied her for a moment. Stacy had gorgeous, heavy red hair that made her fine features seem all the more delicate. Tonight her hair was piled up high with long, loose pieces curling softly around her face. She looked beautiful and old-fashioned—just like she had last week. I knew what Stacy was doing—the same thing I did when an editor asked me to revise something I didn't want to change—fooling with it here and there, but keeping it basically the same.

14

"Come on and show Grandpa," I invited. "We're having dinner. He's setting you a place."

"I can't eat. I've got to fit into my dress."

"Veggies won't hurt you."

She followed me through the dining room and into the kitchen. "Hi, Grandpa."

"Some hair!" he exclaimed.

"Do you like this style?" she asked hopefully.

"I'd like you bald," he replied.

She refused the soup he offered her but sat down between us, the three of us in a row, like people at a counter. After thirty seconds of Grandpa and me slurping, Stacy reached for the fresh-baked bread, pulled off a big hunk of it, and slathered it with butter. I glanced sideways at her.

"I'm eating just half the meal," she explained.

I leaned back on my chair, opened the fridge, and stretched to get the jar of raspberry jam. I'd never understand the way Stacy thinks and she'd never understand me, but we knew each other down to the smallest quirk—and she had always been a sucker for raspberries.

She globbed the jam on her bread and murmured contently, "I needed this."

"So what's going on?" Grandpa asked. "Linda said there was some problem."

"A problem with a happy ending," she replied, turning to me. "You know, you were so nice about the bridesmaid thing, Daisy. And you were right—nine bridesmaids would probably have been one too many."

Three would have been too many if I'd been the third one, but I didn't say that aloud. "You've got a million friends, Stacy. I'm glad your best girlfriends are going to do it. It's like the final celebration for all your sleep-over parties."

"Do you remember my good friend Karen?"

"The matron of honor," I replied, scooping up in my spoon a large amount of broth and vegetables.

"She's pregnant."

"Cool," I said, then started to swallow a steaming mouthful.

"Would you take her place?"

I choked.

"Got to watch out for those lima beans," Grandpa said, although he knew the beans weren't responsible for my gagging.

"Can't you just let out the dress?" I asked when I'd recovered.

"Karen's having some difficulties and needs to stay off her feet," Stacy explained.

"Then why don't you have one of the other bridesmaids do it?" I reasoned.

"I don't want to show favoritism. I've known Karen longer than the others, so they understood why I chose her. And they'd understand why I'd choose you since I don't have a sister and you're my only cousin."

"Oh."

"You're about a size smaller than Karen, so the seamstress will be able to refit the dress," she went on. "Say yes, Daisy! I'd be so glad to have you up there with me on my big day."

16

"Yes," I croaked.

She gave me a hug. "It'll be terrific fun. The reception. The rehearsal dinner. The party this weekend!"

"Party?"

"I hope you don't have any plans for Saturday night."

Grandpa and I glanced at each other. We had tickets to the Orioles game, and Bob Danner, who'd started pitching before I was born, was going for win number three hundred, a major milestone in baseball. There was going to be national TV coverage and all kinds of old sports stars there. Grandpa and I had box seats.

"It's a prewedding party for Mr. Clarke's business associates. The only attendants invited are the maid of honor and the best man," Stacy went on. "But Karen was bringing her husband, so if you want to bring Daniel, I'm sure that would be all right with Travis and his father."

Daniel was a guy I'd met last summer at a camp outside Washington, D.C., where we'd both worked as counselors. The distance between our homes in D.C. and Baltimore was too far for steady dating—and neither of us wanted that anyway—but we kept in touch by E-mail. Actually, I'd usually E-mail *him*—sometimes he'd respond and sometimes he wouldn't. That was just the kind of guy he was. But since I wasn't interested in anyone at school, I'd asked Daniel to the wedding as well as our school dance, which was the last weekend in April.

"It's not really a family thing, Grandpa," Stacy added apologetically.

"Then do you think I should go?" I asked, trying not to sound too hopeful.

"Definitely. I'm not going to know many of the guests. They're the Clarkes' business associates and friends and, well, the kind of people you see in the society page of the *Sun*. I'd feel so much better with you around, Daisy Jane."

What could I say? Since Stacy had started college, we hadn't seen very much of each other, especially in the last year, when Travis had come into her life. But neither of us had siblings or other first cousins, and we'd spent our childhoods together. I was the closest thing she had to a sister.

"Sure," I told her, "I'll come—without a date." Why torture anyone else? *Maybe Danner will have a bad night and delay his three-hundredth win,* I thought.

For the rest of the meal Stacy talked happily about the honeymoon plans, down to the smallest detail. By the time we were finished, I could've led tours of the cruise ship they were going on.

Stacy glanced at her watch. "Oh, no, I was supposed to meet Travis twenty minutes ago to show him my hair."

"Tell him I think it's perfect," I said.

Grandpa rose to walk her to the front door, and I began clearing the dishes. I scraped food from our plates and bowls, hovering longer than necessary over the garbage disposal, watching it grind up pea pods as if each one were a ticket to Saturday's game. I didn't hear my grandfather return and jumped when he spoke from the kitchen doorway.

"Tough decision."

"Yup," I replied.

"One tough girl, our Daisy Jane. Sweet too."

"Don't make me cry," I told him, then laughed a little. "Well, I'd better call Marnie and tell her to cancel her date for Saturday. She's got a hot one with my grandpa."

THREE

"**Y**ES!"
      Marnie's house was three blocks from ours, but I knew exactly where she was standing when I called to tell her she could have my ticket. I could hear Bosco barking the way the little dog always did when someone got her excited and she started running circles around the dining-room table. Eight-year-old Teddy, who usually did his homework there, was complaining loudly, "Don't beat on my head, Marn! Don't beat on my head."

"Yes, yes, yes," Marnie's voice sang through the phone. "Oh, wait a minute, maybe I should ask first why you can't go—have you caught some kind of deadly disease?"

"Yeah. Maid of honorhood."

"What?"

I lay back on my bed, putting my bare feet up against the wall, and explained the situation.

"So," Marnie said, "does this mean you'll have to carry Stacy's train and eat at the long table that faces the guests so everyone knows when you're using the wrong fork?"

"I guess so."

"What are you going to do with Daniel?" she asked.

"What do you mean?"

"I'm pretty sure he can't sit at the bride and groom's table," Marnie explained. "And to be honest, I don't think you want him to."

Marnie had met Daniel twice, once on a double date we'd arranged here in Baltimore and another time on a museum trip to D.C., with the same result both times. He talked to me, then she talked to me, then he, then she—but they had nothing to say to each other. Daniel *was* kind of offbeat and liked people to think of him that way. I think he said some of his crazier things just to get a reaction, but at least he was interesting. What I liked best about him was that he didn't get hung up on fitting in and doing what everybody else was doing. I guess it was the artist in him.

"You think he might not dress right for a wedding?" I asked, sliding my feet down the wall.

"Does he own a tie? Does he own a shirt with a collar?"

"Probably not," I admitted, rolling off my bed. "Well, I guess you're right. It's better if he doesn't sit at the head table. He can just mingle."

Marnie hooted. "Mingle? Daniel? With the friends of Travis Avery Clarke III?"

"Stop laughing, Marnie. Why are you so hard on him?"

"I don't know. He can be intriguing—if you like artist types—but I guess he's not what I'd pick out for you."

"Is there someone on that long list of yours you'd recommend?" I asked.

Marnie dated a lot. She was "a big girl" as my mom would say, tall and strong and blond, and had a big laugh to go with her size. "Every guy's pal, no guy's passion"—that's how Marnie described herself, but even if she'd never had a special guy, she'd had an awful lot of dates. And she was never too shy to ask a guy out.

"You should go out with a jock," Marnie said. "I'm a jock. You like me."

"Yeah, but you know how to talk about something other than the great play you made in the last game and your history of athletic injuries," I replied. "Every time I've been out with a guy jock, he's bored me to death."

"Still, some are awfully cute," she persisted. "Like the one who is sending you fan mail."

"Oh, him." I began to pace around my room.

"Yeah, him. You two should say nicer things about each other since you're alike in so many ways."

"Excuse me?" I dropped down on my desk chair and rocked back on it.

"Think about it. You're both stubborn, determined types," Marnie pointed out. "And you both love sports. Plus you've got to admit," she added, "Adam can write!"

"Yeah, well, you can talk about that with Grandpa on Saturday night while you're watching baseball history being made and I'm walking around eating little finger foodies with people from the society page."

She laughed, then said good-bye. I stood up, clicked off my phone, and tossed it onto my bed.

While we were talking, the last bit of daylight had disappeared. I love clear April nights, when it's too dark to see the flowers but you can still smell springtime—its dense, earthy scent and the heady fragrance of blossoms that seems to float above it. I knelt by my window and pushed it all the way up so I could lean out.

I had a ton of assignments to finish tonight, as well as an E-mail to send to Daniel. I wanted to warn him about my official role in the wedding as well as remind him about our school's spring dance, which was the week before.

But for a few minutes I stayed at the window, listening to the rustle of delicate leaves, feeling the evening air soft on my bare arms. There's a gentleness about April that made me ache. It seemed like I was always on the run, always working and chasing some goal or another, but April had a way of holding me still. And then I'd begin to hurt and yearn for something I couldn't describe, something I hadn't known yet. All I knew was the ache itself and the strange, sweet feeling it was.

"Keep it moving! Keep it moving!"
"Jeez, you brought your man to him! Middies, where you cutting?"

23

"Hustle, hustle, hustle!"

The coaches from both teams were yelling. We had one minute to go and the game was tied. We were playing first-ranked Gilman and had a chance to better our record to 4–3. This could be a big win. I was flipping pages and writing without glancing down—notes only I could read. I had the father of a player on one side of me and Marnie on the other, both of them hollering their lungs out with the rest of the home-team crowd. Vinny was standing behind me, one bleacher step up, beating on my back. I'd given up telling him that a writer can't get caught up in the emotion of a game; a reporter has to stay cool like a player, aware of every corner of the field, thinking through the game as the players do.

"Come on, Adam!" Marnie and Vinny shouted together as Logan gave a little shoulder fake, dodged his defensemen, and made a sharp pass to the crease attack. The attackman quick-sticked it but missed the goal.

"Try it again!" Marnie shouted. "You can do it, Tilson!"

Our coach, Mr. Gryczgowski, better known as "Grizzly"—though not to his face—was leaping around the sidelines like a bear dancing to hip-hop. Sometimes he got so excited that the guys had to pull him back from the sideline so he wouldn't step into the game.

Out of the corner of my eye I saw Grizzly's arms suddenly go up to his head, as if he wanted to smother himself. The home crowd groaned. A penalty was called against us for a stupid mistake: Our player had stepped into the crease.

"The turnovers are killing us," I said as the other team cleared the ball up the field.

"We can hold 'em," Marnie replied, "then beat them in overtime."

"Come on, defense. Slide!" I hollered in spite of my resolve to remain cool. "Get him!"

In five seconds it was over. The Gilman player face-dodged, then bounced the ball in. Gilman's sticks shot up in triumph. The silence in our part of the stands was deafening.

"Okay, Vin," I said dejectedly. "Time to ask questions." He followed me slowly out of the stands. "I wish we didn't have to interview the guys when we lose."

I glanced back at him. Vinny's eyebrows were pulled together in a worried expression. He'd told Tom he wanted to cover sports, but I had the feeling he'd be more at ease doing cheerful, bland features with Kelly.

The players formed lines and shook the hands of their opponents. Vinny and I stood on the sidelines, him shifting from foot to foot, me trying to make a quick count of turnovers. I caught hold of Roger, the team manager, as he tried to slip by. He kept the stats, so I was always bugging him.

"Our shooting percentage is high this week, Jane. That would be a good thing to focus on."

"Right, I've got that," I said. "What I need is the breakdown of our offensive and defensive turnovers, and while you're at it, the percentage of ground balls we recovered."

Roger sighed, did some calculating, and gave me the numbers. "Of course, they don't tell the whole story," he reminded me.

"And what would you say is the story?"

"Adam Logan—equal to the best of the best in the league," he said.

I nodded. "I'd say that's one of them." I turned to Vinny. "Who do you want to interview, Josh or Adam?" Josh, as goalie, was the leader of the defense.

"Josh," Vinny said. "I don't think he can put together a sentence, so he probably can't write a letter to the editor."

Josh liked to give that impression—he liked people to think he was a no-brain guy, a madman out there ready to eat eighty-mile-per-hour balls. But I knew better. He was as fast mentally as he was physically and always gave me good quotes.

"Okay, go to it," I told Vinny. I had to wait to get to Adam since he was surrounded by team supporters. Lacrosse was a popular sport in Maryland and always drew a big crowd, but I think our team captain had won over even more fans than usual, especially the girls in our school.

While I was waiting, I called out to one of our attackmen. "Hey, Ryan, got a minute?"

"Nope," he called back.

I gazed after him with surprise, then circled around Adam's crowd.

"Hi, Jordy," I said. "I have some questions for you."

"Maybe Adam will answer them," he told me, and headed off.

"Pablo?"

"Later," he said.

I was getting the cold shoulder. I tried three more players with the same results. What if I couldn't get anything for the column? I didn't believe in writing articles without the subjects' input. Jimmy Olsten's granddaughter gritted her teeth, more determined than ever, but Daisy Jane was getting her feelings hurt.

I made my way toward Adam. "Hi, I've got some questions," I told him. He didn't say anything—just picked up his stick and helmet, tucked his gloves under his arm, and started walking.

"You wouldn't mind answering them, would you?"

"I'll answer any reasonable questions," he replied as he wove his way through the crowd. People were patting him on the back, saying encouraging things to him. I struggled to keep up with him.

"Nice shot just before halftime," I told him.

I could see his hand tighten on his stick.

"Hey, Adam, great effort!" a fan called.

"Adam, you were awesome!"

He nodded at the two girls. "Thanks for coming."

"And it was a good assist after the face-off," I added as we made our way between the bleachers.

His grip on the stick tightened again.

"Do I make you tense?" I asked.

"When you flatter me before moving in for the kill, yes."

27

"That wasn't flattery," I replied, "it was the truth."

He swung around and faced me, his eyes such a brilliant green, they were all I saw. "The truth is that the guy assigned to me overcommitted himself and made it easy." He started walking again.

I flipped open my notebook and scribbled down his words. They were honest and modest, but not the entire truth.

"Of course," I said, walking fast, paging backward in my book to see what I'd jotted down during the game, "that guy overcommitted because in the previous offensive play, you drove in hard from the right side, setting him up so he had to go after you the next time."

Adam glanced down at me, his eyes wary.

"Am I right?"

"This time," he replied.

We crossed a bridge that spanned the stream between the upper athletic fields and lower. Several girls were sitting on the railing, dangling their long, bare legs. I could smell the suntan lotion. "Hey, Adam," they greeted him.

"Give me a call tonight," one of them said. I kept quiet till we were well beyond the bridge. Girls with silky-soft voices always made me self-conscious.

As we started across the baseball field, Adam turned to me. "How about asking what's really on your mind so I can go take a shower?"

"You trying to get rid of me?"

"Yes."

I was getting annoyed. I tried for a moment to

28

see him through other people's eyes, through the eyes of the girls on the bridge. His blond hair, still wet with perspiration, curled around the edge of his face and back of his neck. His lashes looked thick and golden against his green eyes. A sheen of sweat highlighted his high cheekbones and strong jawline. He had everything going for him, looks, brains, athletic talent, and yet—

"Why do I bother you so much?" I asked bluntly. "There are a horde of people in this school who'll tell you what fast moves you have, what a bulletlike shot, sexy body, and great face—"

"What?" he asked, leaning down close as if he'd missed what I said.

"You heard me."

He straightened up. "Is this a question for your column?"

"It's something I've been trying to figure out. Why do you get hot and bothered by one person's opinion, especially when everyone else treats you like a hero? I mean, you had to be pretty irritated to write three columns about me."

"Four—I cut it back," he said, quickening his pace. "The answer is, I don't know. Next question."

"We got half the face-offs today, which is better than previous weeks. Any comment?"

"No, but I'm sure you've got one."

Okay, I thought, *if he doesn't want to talk about the positive stuff, I'll give him something else.* "We recovered less than forty percent of the ground balls. What do you think about that?"

"Same thing you do, probably," he said. "Next question."

"There were eight turnovers in the first half, when you were playing a 2-1-1-2 offense, and five in the second half, when, for the most part, you played the standard 2-1-3. In the second half you got off twice as many shots. Want to talk about that?"

"I'd have to say we played better in the second half. Next question?"

I bit my tongue. *Keep cool,* I told myself, *keep cool.*

"Next question," he prompted. "You've got between here and the school door."

"Give me a break!"

"Funny, that's something I've wanted from you for a long time."

"Listen, Logan," I replied. "You get out your highlighter and go through my columns and you'll see I've said plenty of good stuff about you and your teammates. But I'm not a cheerleader. I'm a writer, and my job is to give people who are reading the paper a clear picture."

"Of things as *you* see them," he said.

"Some of you guys have awfully tender little egos."

"At least I don't have your big one," he answered. "I don't assume that I see things the only way they can be seen. I don't write like I know all about a sport I can't even play."

We glared at each other.

"Any further questions?" he asked.

"Why waste my time?" I replied.

"At least we agree on something," he said, then walked off.

FOUR

"WANT TO TALK about it?" Grandpa asked me Saturday afternoon as we did garden work in our backyard.

"Maybe."

It was unusually warm for April, with the temperatures rising into the eighties. We both wore shorts, and I'd put on a tank top with a deep-scooped neck, hoping to start a tan. Grandpa planted poppies along the fence that bordered the back alley, his big hands working slowly, patiently with the delicate seeds, while I viciously attacked some weeds.

It had taken me a while to sort out yesterday's postgame scene, and I'd always preferred to keep things to myself until I'd thought them through. But the more I thought, the more I got stuck on the very same question I'd asked Adam: Why did one person's opinion of me get me hot and bothered?

Other people had said I was doing a great job.

Tom thought so. Some of the teachers I really respected had said positive things about my writing. Last year I'd won a citywide award for a series on soccer. How many pats on the back did I need?

After Vinny had interviewed Josh yesterday, Josh caught up with me outside the locker room. He said Vinny hadn't hit him with the kind of questions I usually asked, and then, without any prompting, he gave me some great quotes. Coach came by and added several helpful insights. As for the guys who had given me the cold shoulder, they were probably just following Adam's lead. So why couldn't I just write off Adam as a jerk?

"Grandpa, did you ever question yourself as a writer?"

He held a palmful of seeds and gazed at me intently.

"I mean, did you ever wonder if you were seeing things correctly?"

"In the beginning, all the time," he said. "When I was an old pro, every three months."

I groaned. "I was hoping this was just a phase I was going through."

I recounted Friday's events, and Grandpa listened as he worked. "So, what do you think?" I asked at last.

"I think you still haven't trained Vinny, but you've done a fine job with Josh."

I laughed. "Josh is okay—and Adam's best friend, believe it or not."

"His best friend, and yet he's not taking things personally," Grandpa pointed out. "That's something to keep in mind."

I nodded.

"Looking back," Grandpa continued, "sometimes I was right and sometimes I was wrong. I wrote as I saw and tried my hardest to see different sides. The only thing I know for sure, Jane, is that it's the reporters who never question themselves that I worry about."

I crawled over to the next set of weeds and started pulling again, feeling a little better. The sun was growing hot and felt good on my back and arms. Grandpa had brought out the radio and turned on the Orioles game. Other people were working in their yards, and another radio echoed the game several gardens down. Saturday-afternoon opera floated down from a higher window across the alley, probably Mrs. Bean's. I glanced up to see our neighbor observing us from her second-floor perch.

"Your secret admirer is watching you, Grandpa."

"And who would that be?" he asked without looking up.

A widow in her late fifties, Mrs. Bean had always had an eye for Grandpa. She lived in one of the two big end houses that bookended a cluster of five smaller houses directly across the alley from us. She had a good-size third floor, a side yard, and a garage facing the alley, whose gable was an ideal place to mount a basketball hoop. I sometimes thought she'd left up her rim as a lure to Grandpa, who'd still shoot baskets with me.

I waved up at her, then turned toward the alley to see whose truck was rumbling over the potholes.

A U-Haul parked in front of Mrs. Bean's, and another car pulled up behind the rental truck.

"Never mind, it's not you she's waiting for after all," I said, noticing that our neighbor had disappeared from the upstairs window.

Grandpa raised his head just enough to see the truck. "Guess she's renting out again," he grunted. "Found herself another fellow to do yard work."

"Looks like it. Oh my gosh!"

Grandpa straightened up. "What?"

I nodded toward the tall man who'd just gotten out of the truck. "It's Coach Gryczgowski."

Four guys from the lacrosse team got out of the car and gathered around him, all of them watching Mrs. Bean coming down the back walk in her black leggings and big flower top.

Grandpa stood up. "Is your number-one fan among the moving crew?"

I nodded and pointed out Adam, then Josh, who was standing next to him. Pablo, another midfielder, and Billy, a defenseman, had also come.

It didn't take long for Mrs. Bean to notice Grandpa watching. "Hel-loo, neighbors!" she called. "Come on over and meet my new tenant."

The guys turned around to see who she was waving at. Adam's friendly expression froze. Pablo and Billy glanced sideways at him. Josh grinned.

"Everyone, this is Jimmy Olsten and his granddaughter, Jane," Mrs. Bean announced as we entered the alley.

"*The* Jimmy Olsten?" Grizzly's clean-shaven

face grew bright, then broke into a huge grin.

"Actually, my last name is Olstenheimer," Grandpa told him, "but that was long for a byline."

"I can't believe it!" Grizzly exclaimed, his brown eyes opening wide. "I can't believe I'm finally meeting you." He shook Grandpa's hand enthusiastically, then glanced at me. "You never mentioned Jimmy Olsten was your grandfather."

"I earn my own way."

"Guys," he said to his team, "I used to read this man's sports columns every day in the *Sun*. Heck, I still have some of them—I have one with a paragraph you wrote about me," he added, sounding suddenly shy. "He wrote great stuff," Coach went on to his team, "exciting stuff, and started a few arguments along the way." Then Grizzly looked at me and grinned again, as if he suddenly saw the resemblance.

Grizzly turned back to Grandpa. "I read you before you went to *Sports Illustrated* and was really glad when you came back to the *Sun*," he added. "But I've always wondered why you gave up the big time."

Grandpa shrugged. "I liked the local scene. I missed my old teams."

"That's how it is in Baltimore," Grizzly agreed. "I still miss the Colts. Do you remember the week before the Colts left town, back in 1984, when you found out that—"

They were heading down memory lane—those conversations could go on indefinitely between sports fans. As soon as Grandpa and Coach paused for breath, Adam interjected, "We'll start to unload, Coach."

"Need some help?" I offered, following the guys to the back of the truck.

"Nope," Adam replied.

"Sure," Josh said. "We can always use help."

"I don't think so," Adam told his friend. "It's heavy stuff."

"Don't worry. I'll find something my dainty little arms can manage," I said to Adam. The other three guys snickered.

Coach had cartons of books and a jumble of furniture that must've been Salvation Army specials. While Grizzly chatted with Grandpa, Mrs. Bean directed us, though she had no more idea than we did where her new tenant wanted things. There were just two rooms to choose between on the third floor, the one to the left of the steps and the one to the right. The bathroom was at the top of the stairway. A microwave and small fridge were all Coach had for a kitchen.

After ten minutes of lugging stuff up the front steps, then struggling with it for two more flights after that and ending up on the stuffy third floor, all of us were sweating. The guys took off their T-shirts, much to the delight of Mrs. Bean. I could've made fun of her, but I found myself appreciating Adam from behind, studying the width of his shoulders and the hard muscles that rippled in his back when he lifted a bookcase and carried it up the steps ahead of me. For one moment I wondered what it would be like to put my arms around a back like his.

Of course, after he put down the bookcase and

36

turned around, there was that same old stony face. It was pointless to try to make conversation, so I headed downstairs, flattening myself against the wall when Pablo and Billy carried a mattress by me, Coach following with the bed frame.

When I got to the alley, Grandpa had gone back to gardening. Josh was sitting on a banged-up bureau. "Will you give me a hand with this?" he asked, hopping off. "It's not heavy, just awkward."

"No problem," I said. That was before I tried to lift it. For me it was very heavy, but there was no way I'd admit that to him.

We tried various grips until we got ourselves comfortable, me on the front end, walking forward, my hands grasping the bureau behind me, and Josh bringing up the rear, making sure the bureau stayed upright. We were at the main entrance on the side of the house when Adam passed by.

"Adam, great timing!" Josh said. "Take the end, okay?"

I was sure that he meant for him to take my place, but instead Josh handed Adam his own end. Now I'd have to die before admitting the task was too much for me. Adam and I watched Josh walk away, as if neither of us could believe we were stuck with each other carrying this thing.

"Are you leading or am I supposed to be pushing?" Adam asked.

"I'm leading. Let's go."

We struggled to get it up the front steps and through the hall without taking Mrs. Bean's door hinges and wallpaper with us. After pausing for a moment to catch our breath, we started up the first big flight of steps. We were halfway up when the weight behind me suddenly shifted. We careened sideways, crashing against the wall. I heard Adam spit out a word, then try to disguise it as *shoot*.

"What are you doing?" I asked, my voice hoarse from strain.

"What am I doing?" he replied incredulously. "You just tipped it."

"I did not."

"You did so."

"What's Coach got inside this old thing?" I asked.

"Clothes," he said. "Keep going. I'm bearing the weight of this, remember?"

We worked to get ourselves upright, took two steps more, then careened toward the other side.

"I didn't do it!" we both said at the same time.

"I think he's got a bowling ball rolling around in here."

"Coach doesn't bowl," Adam replied, then we struggled on.

By the time we got to the second floor, we were both drenched with sweat.

"I'm going to have to walk backward," I said. "The next set is steeper, and I'm losing my grip."

We stopped and I turned around slowly till we were facing each other over the bureau.

"You okay?" he asked, his voice a little gentler.

"Yes." My legs were wobbly and my arms felt four inches longer than their natural size, but I'd have to be lying crushed under the bureau before I asked for assistance.

"Take it easy. Take it one step at a time," he said.

The edge of his hair was curling up with sweat as it did during a game. I could feel strands of mine pasted against my face. We made our way slowly up the second and narrower set of steps.

"I can't see where I'm going," I said as I climbed the steps backward, the bureau up against my ribs, me leaning over the top of it. "You've got to do the steering, okay?

"Okay?" I repeated a moment later, when my elbow bumped the wall. "Are you watching where we're going?" I glanced across the bureau at him, meeting his eyes as they darted up to mine. He'd been watching my chest! When I looked down at myself and saw the view Adam had been getting, I nearly dropped the bureau.

"Hold on!" he shouted at me. For a moment it wasn't clear which of us had a grip. "Jane! Hold on! Are you trying to kill me?"

I would've shouted back, but I was too exhausted. Besides, Adam was blushing, something I'd never seen him do before.

"Okay," I said, "let's get this over with."

We grunted, lifted, and heaved until the bureau was finally sitting level on the third floor. Together we shoved it against one of the sloping walls. I collapsed next to it, leaning back against the wall the way I did in my own room. Adam bent over the bureau, perhaps so he didn't have to look me in the eye, and started pulling off the tape that secured the drawers. He opened one and peeked in it, then the next.

"Looking for a bowling ball?" I asked.

"I don't get it," he muttered, then opened a third. "I don't understand why this was so—"

A big, furry thing leaped out.

"Yikes!" I said.

Adam straightened up quickly and banged his head hard on the sloping ceiling. He rubbed his head, hissing out several words and making no attempt to disguise them.

An overweight gray-and-white cat had landed about two feet away from him. It switched its tail back and forth, watching Adam with feline amusement. I couldn't help it—I started laughing.

Josh's head appeared as he climbed the steps to our level. "Hey, it's Big Mama!" Josh exclaimed. "Coach, we've found Big Mama."

Grizzly hurried up the steps behind Josh. "There's my girl!" he said, sounding greatly relieved. "Where have you been? I didn't know what had happened to you, sweetie."

Sweetie?

"She was trapped in the bureau, Coach," Adam told him.

"Poor Big Mama," Grizzly murmured, stooping and stroking the cat very gently. He picked her up, putting her over his shoulder like she was a baby that needed burping. I knew Coach got emotional about games, but I hadn't expected to see this kind of tenderness toward an obese cat.

Pablo and Billy came up the steps, saw Coach with his cat, and grinned at each other.

"Time to meet Mrs. Bean," Grizzly said, then carried the cat downstairs.

"Thank God," Pablo remarked. "Now we don't have to run through Grizzly's old neighborhood yelling, *'Big Mama, Big Mama.'*"

I reached for the edge of the bureau and pulled myself up from the floor. "Well, it's been fun. Got to go," I said.

"Why, so you can get started on your column?" Billy asked, flopping down in a chair.

"No, I'm doing that tomorrow."

Josh stretched out on the floor, and Pablo dropped down beside him. "What are you going to say?" Pablo asked.

"Her usual," Adam replied before I could. "What does it matter?"

"I'd say it matters a lot to you," I retorted, "though I don't know why."

There was a moment of silence as everyone looked at him for the answer.

"What you think doesn't mean a thing—not to me, Jane. But what makes me mad is the way you can sit back and spin your theories, tell everybody what we're doing wrong, how we need leadership, et cetera, et cetera, when you're not out there running your butt off and getting sticks in your face—when you're not being taken out by a player coming at you full speed or having a hard ball hurled at you at eighty miles per hour. Seems

41

to me it's just a little too easy for you writers."

"I know the sport is difficult."

"Do you?" He leaned back against the bureau and folded his arms, looking at me steadily.

Now, I wasn't so caught up in sports that I didn't recognize a gorgeous guy when I saw one, especially one that was naked from the waist up. But I wasn't so caught up in guys that I couldn't keep my mind on the argument.

"I've followed lacrosse since I was three and my grandfather was taking me to games at Homewood Field. And I've played it."

"Against all-metro players?" he asked.

"Against someone like Adam?" Pablo chimed in.

"Take her on!" Billy said. "One-on-one, Adam. Show her how easy it is to play at our level."

Adam held up his hands. "Not a good idea."

"Why not?" I asked.

"Come on," he said, "it would be a joke."

"I have a sense of humor," I told him, "and you can work on yours."

He grimaced.

"Let's do it," Billy said. "Monday afternoon, four-fifteen. Coach has to leave practice early," he reminded his teammates.

I knew it was a crazy thing to do. I still owned a stick and played one-on-one with Marnie, but I hadn't worked out with a team since middle school. I glanced at Josh, who had stayed quiet during the discussion.

"Is it worth it to you, Jane?" he asked.

"If it ends this stupid cold-shoulder stuff, yes," I replied. "Here's the deal. I won't whine when you teach me a thing or two Monday if you all don't whine when I write a thing or two after that. Agreed?"

Pablo and Billy nodded, then glanced at Adam.

"Got a problem?" I asked when he didn't say anything.

"No problem," he replied.

For you, maybe, I thought as I left. What had I gotten myself into?

FIVE

THREE HOURS LATER, when I was ready to leave for the Clarkes' party, I looked like a totally different person. Stacy had lent me a short, fitted dress made of red silk. "It'll look good with your dark coloring," she'd said, gazing down at the dress longingly. Travis wouldn't let her wear it because he thought it clashed with her hair.

When my mother saw me in Stacy's dress and power heels, she got a worried expression. "Remember, you're in high school," she said.

"Like I'm going to pick up some old lawyer?" I laughed and gave her a hug. "Make sure the VCR clicks on at game time."

Grandpa and Marnie had already left for Camden Yards to see baseball history being made. I drove to the country club where the Clarkes were members, listening to the Orioles' pregame show and sighing a lot. Any hope of staying in the car long enough to

44

catch the first inning quickly vanished. As soon as I pulled through the club's gates, valets swarmed the car, insisting on parking it for me.

The old club was built like a southern mansion, with a long veranda and pillars across the front. Two couples walked up the steps as if they knew where they were going. I followed them, but when I got inside the foyer, there were several archways to choose from. A waiter in a tux asked the name of my host, then led me down thickly carpeted steps.

The party was in a large, private room with two chandeliers and glass doors that opened out to a balcony. I took one step inside the entrance, then stopped and looked for someone familiar—Stacy, Aunt Susan, Uncle Jake. Even Travis, who I barely knew and barely liked, would've been a welcome sight. But all I saw were a lot of well-dressed, frosted-haired women and matching gray-haired men.

"Are you sure this is the Clarkes' party?" I asked the waiter.

"Yes, miss."

Well, I guess the only thing I can do is eat, I thought, and headed for a long table where other tuxedoed men were serving guests. One offered me a plate, and I started browsing. Multicolored sushi was laid out on trays like big buttons next to a large, glassy-eyed fish that looked about as happy as me to be there. I was so fascinated by the fish, I missed the miniature crab cakes, which was what I really wanted. Backtracking suddenly, I bumped into someone. "Sorry."

45

The person I'd bumped leaned far to the right, as if trying to peer around me. I stepped aside so he could get by.

"Jane?" he asked with disbelief in his voice.

I turned quickly. *His* was not the familiar face I was hoping to see.

Adam was a picture of amazement. "Jane?" he repeated.

"Well, who do you think it is?" I said. "Do I look that different after a bath?"

"Yes," he replied honestly. "What are you doing here?"

"I was invited."

"By whom?" he wanted to know.

"The bride," I said. "Stacy Olstenheimer, as in Jimmy Olstenheimer. Do you work here?" I asked, observing his formal wear. I should have noticed that the jacket was a different cut from the waiters', but I was too busy noticing how he looked in it—really good.

One side of Adam's mouth pulled up in a wry smile. "No, I'm a guest. Travis is my stepbrother."

"But your last name is—oh, Mr. Clarke is your stepfather."

Adam nodded.

"Well—well, you look better after a bath too," I told him.

He gave me a smirky smile.

"So, all these people here are business associates?" I asked. "None of them are actually in the wedding?"

"Except me. My stepfather thought I should be

the best man." Maybe Adam saw the dazed expression on my face.

"You know, the guy who stands next to the groom at the altar," he added, "the guy who calms him down, holds the ring—"

"Walks the maid of honor down the aisle," I said.

"Right."

"I'm the maid of honor."

For a moment he didn't respond.

"Stacy's original choice had to drop out," I explained, "so I was drafted. Believe me, I didn't volunteer for this. I had a ticket to Bob Danner's three-hundredth win tonight."

"But what happened to Stacy's cousin, crazy Daisy?" he asked.

I hesitated. "She grew up."

"You mean you're Daisy?" He burst out laughing.

"It's not that funny a name," I said, moving away from him and helping myself to some food.

"I'm not laughing at the name," he replied, following behind, "I'm laughing at the stories I've heard about you."

"Like what?" I demanded, although I knew my family had an anthology of Daisy tales.

He shrugged. "There were a lot of them. The time you talked timid little Stacy into going in the haunted house, the walk-in type, and you didn't come out at the end."

"Oh, that."

"The time you told her you had some disease so you wouldn't have to share your dessert and were so convincing she had all the kids in her class pray for you."

And raise money, I thought. Aloud I said, "Stacy has always had an active imagination. Most of the opportunities were just too hard to pass up."

"I bet," he replied, moving along with me, still grinning. I guessed it was an improvement over the cold-shoulder routine.

But the old coolness returned when we reached the end of the buffet. A waiter told Adam that Mr. Clarke wanted to see him. Adam glanced in the direction of the balcony doors, then turned to me, suddenly stiff.

"Well, party down," he said, the laughter completely gone now, not even a smirky smile to lighten his face.

I watched him make his way across the room to the French doors, puzzled by his abrupt change in mood. This time it wasn't something I'd said that had irritated him, so there was nothing I could do about it. I snuck back in line to get two more crab cakes, then headed off to find my own family, nibbling as I walked.

As it turned out, I came upon Aunt Susan and Uncle Jake by those same French doors. They were watching Stacy and Travis on the balcony as they were being posed and photographed. My aunt and uncle beamed with love and pride, an expression that made me think of other family events like Stacy's piano and ballet recitals, her birthday parties and graduations. I found myself smiling with them.

"She looks so pretty," I whispered as I joined them.

"Daisy," they said softly, each of them putting an arm around me.

Adam was also watching the photo shoot. He turned and glanced at me, then the woman next to him turned toward us. When I saw her green eyes, I knew instantly she was his mother. She smiled and nudged the tall, gray-haired man next to her, but he was too intent on watching the photographer and telling him what to do.

"Is that Mr. Clarke?" I asked quietly.

My aunt and uncle nodded.

"How about Travis's mother—is she here?"

My aunt shook her head. "They didn't invite her to the wedding. She left Mr. Clarke when Travis was very young. That's the new Mrs. Clarke, who married Avery after her own husband died, five or six years ago."

As we talked, an old man with mischievous eyes and large ears approached Adam and whispered something to him. Adam grinned in response, then followed the elflike gentleman across the room. Mrs. Clarke watched her son for a moment, then came over to me to be introduced. She was a warm lady with a quiet voice. She called to her husband twice. After a few more instructions to the photographer, Mr. Clarke joined us.

"Jane Hardy," he repeated, and looked at me like a legal case he was trying to remember. "Why is that name so familiar? Do you go to public school?"

It seemed an odd question. "Yes," I replied. "Tilson High."

"Really," said Mrs. Clarke. "My son, Adam—"

Mr. Clarke cut her off. "And you write for the newspaper. You cover the lacrosse team."

"That's right." I liked being recognized. Aunt Susan and Uncle Jake beamed at me as they had at Stacy.

"Is the team still playing below its ability?" Mr. Clarke inquired.

"Well, uh—"

"What's holding them back?" he asked before I could answer the first question. "The newfangled plays by that young coach? Are the decoys still leaving us with sitting ducks?"

I blinked. It was weird to hear myself quoted. His last question had been one of my best leads— "When decoys make us nothing but sitting ducks," I'd written, "it's time to return to basic lacrosse."

"There's nothing worse than watching a team with talent lose one close game after another," Mr. Clarke went on. "Where's their fight? Talent is worth nothing if you can't execute. If Adam isn't doing his job, if he's not leading the others, then the coach needs to find someone else who will."

It seemed an awfully harsh thing for a family member to say—although, essentially, it was what I had said.

"I'm curious to know what you think," I told him. "How does the team look to you?"

"I've never seen them."

"Avery is so busy these days," Mrs. Clarke interjected, her hand resting on her husband's arm. "We follow Adam's team through the paper."

"Just through the paper?" I asked. *Just through my eyes?*

"When he was younger, I went to all his games," Mrs. Clarke replied, sounding somewhat defensive. "But we're so busy now."

"So you said."

"And Adam doesn't tell us much," she added.

"Doesn't tell us a thing," Mr. Clarke observed.

"So you rely on *The Pipeline,*" I concluded. No wonder Adam was sensitive to what I wrote. Deep down, everybody cares about their parents' opinion. I mean, my dad was a jerk and I hadn't seen him for five years, but I still wondered whether he'd be proud of me.

There were probably a few other guys on the team whose parents skipped the games and read the paper instead. Things were finally making sense. But what was I supposed to do about it—give everything a positive spin?

I felt bad for Adam, having to deal with an opinionated stepfather who apparently made him accountable for whatever I wrote. And I cringed when I remembered some of the things I'd published. I was furious with Mr. Clarke for being an old bully rather than a supportive parent.

For once, wedding talk came as a relief. As soon as the subject was changed to final preparations for the big day, I put down my plate and bolted. Halfway across the room I passed Adam.

He reached out and caught me by the arm. "Is something wrong?"

"Wrong? Like what?"

"I don't know," he replied. "But you've got that look on your face."

"What look?"

"The one that warns me I'd better get to the showers fast."

My hands went up to my cheeks. I could feel them turning a hot pink. After what I'd just heard, I would have felt better if he'd given me the old cold shoulder, but he looked at me curiously now, as if he were trying to read my thoughts.

"Nothing's wrong," I told him.

"I don't believe you."

"I just need some air," I insisted.

"Okay," he said. I could tell he wasn't convinced. "On your way back in, check out the upstairs cloak-room. Travis's great-uncle snuck in a portable TV."

"He did?" I asked, brightening considerably.

Adam laughed. "The Os are winning three-zip and Danner's allowed just one hit so far."

"Yeah?"

"Yeah." He smiled a gorgeous smile with a surprising edge of shyness.

I hurried upstairs, my heart giving a little skip—because of the Orioles, of course.

SIX

I ARRIVED HOME just after Grandpa and Marnie.
All three of us talked at the same time, intertwining the events of the game and the party. I'd watched
Danner get his big win while sitting with six men
and Adam on the floor of the country-club cloak-
room. Every time the Orioles had made a good play,
Travis's great-uncle had stood up and clanged the
hangers.

That night Marnie slept over. We climbed into
our sleeping bags and lay quietly for a few minutes,
then she turned to me and said, "Fate."

"Hmmm?" I was already drifting off to sleep.

"First Adam shows up in your back alley, then
you're paired up for a wedding. There's some kind
of cosmic force at work."

"You read too many magazines," I told her. "Go
to sleep."

My eyes had just closed a second time when she

asked, "So, are you dreaming about Daniel?"

"Marnie! I was almost asleep."

"Well, are you?" she persisted.

"No."

"Get plenty of rest," she advised. "I'm working you hard tomorrow."

She wasn't kidding. The next day, despite buckets of rain, she drilled me on face-offs, dodges, and defense, getting me ready for Monday's one-on-one match with Adam.

Unfortunately Monday was the girls' game as well. At lunchtime Marnie shared with me her "high-octane" sandwich—peanut butter and apples—fuel for victory, she told me. That afternoon I watched the first two quarters of her game. At halftime she trotted over to give me a last-minute pep talk, then we wished each other good luck and I headed for the guys' field, leaving Vinny behind to cover the girls.

When I got to the other field, I saw that Coach had left early as he'd said he would, but all the players were still there, along with a dozen kids from the newspaper and some of their friends. I'd told Tom and Angela about the deal, asking them to keep it quiet. Later I found out that Kelly had gotten wind of it from one of the players and spread the word.

Angela, Tom, and several others held up a long sign: Hammer Him Hard, Hardy!

"Listen, you guys," I said as I reached them, "you know I haven't got a chance."

"Go, Jane!" was their response.

Adam, who was standing with his buddies about

twenty feet away, glanced over his shoulder at us. I was glad to see that old cold shoulder again. After Saturday night I needed to be reminded why I was about to make a fool of myself. A lot of ribbing and grief were sure to follow; I could handle that, and then the guys' team would have to handle my questions and commentary.

Josh strolled over to me, wearing a whistle around his neck and carrying equipment. "Okay, champ," he said to me, "these are the smallest pads we could find."

In girls' lacrosse only the goalie wears protection. But in the guys' game checking is allowed and the play is much rougher. Equipment is necessary.

The rib pads overlapped on me and had to be belted on. The shoulder protection made me look as if I were ready to sprout wings. The arm and elbow pads weren't too bad, but the padded gloves, which extended about six inches past the wrists of a guy, were huge and loose. Josh put the helmet on my head and tightened the strap. I could see him trying not to laugh.

"How are you feeling?" he asked.

"Like Lancelot."

I picked up my stick and walked to the face-off marker, aware that somebody from the newspaper was taking pictures. I had the feeling an unflattering blowup photo of me would soon be hanging in the *Pipeline*'s office.

Adam met me at the X in the center of the field, looked me up and down in the ill-fitting armor, then said to Josh, who'd followed us out, "I don't think this is a good idea."

"We made a deal," I told him. "I won't whine, then you guys won't whine—remember?"

He grunted his answer and turned to Josh in a confidential manner. "We'll alternate carrying the ball downfield. She can go first."

"Are you kidding?" I exclaimed, sticking my face in between them. "I spent half of yesterday practicing face-offs."

"The team that controls the face-offs controls the game," Adam reminded me. "But you know that—you've mentioned it several times in your columns."

"I also know I haven't much of a chance today. But we'll play the game the way it's supposed to be played."

"Have it your way," he said with a shrug.

"Our way. It was an agreement."

"We'll play one quarter," Josh said, "ten minutes running time."

"Make it five," Adam told him, as if I couldn't survive ten.

"Give me a break!" I said.

"I'm trying to," he replied, "but you're too proud to take it!"

"Talk about pride," I muttered, wondering how we'd gotten along Saturday night. I positioned myself, leaning over at the waist, my hands gripping my stick and spread apart, my knuckles touching the ground. *Start low, stay low,* Marnie had told me. *Keep your head over the ball.*

"I'm ready, ref."

"She makes me crazy," Adam said to Josh, then got in position, bent over and facing me, laying his stick back-to-back with mine. Josh placed the ball between our stick heads, backed away, and whistled the start.

We clamped, we raked, we pushed, we shoved. The field was in bad shape from yesterday's rain, making it difficult to get the ball. Mud flew. My only hope was quickness and the fact that Adam figured I didn't know what I was doing. *He* didn't know that in middle school, face-offs were my specialty.

I scooped the ball.

"Run!" everyone on the newspaper shrieked.

I flew down the field, cradling to keep the ball in the net of my upright stick. I heard Adam coming behind me and switched hands to keep my body between him and my stick. But he was fast. A quick poke check knocked the ball loose.

We both raced after it.

"Ball, ball, ball," the spectators shouted.

Adam was just about to scoop it. I wasn't close enough to scoop, but I could lunge and push it past him. I charged forward to jab the ball. It scooted beyond his stick, then I fell flat on my face. "Oof." I could taste the mud. I felt it seeping into my shorts.

Adam turned back, ignoring the ball for a moment, extending a hand to help me up. I scrambled past him and quickly retrieved the ball.

He couldn't believe it. "You're playing dirty!"

"I'm playing smart. You didn't hear the ref's whistle, did you?"

What wasn't smart was to make him mad. Four minutes later he'd scored three quick goals against me.

I could tell by the light sound of his stick against mine that he wasn't checking as hard as he would in a guys' game, and he was trying to avoid the gloved part of my hand and arm. Even so, I was going to have a million bruises tomorrow, including those of my own making, as we shoved, collided, and fell in the mud. Mostly it was I who fell in the mud.

I watched his eyes and tried to anticipate where he was going. I poked-checked, I slap-checked, but his wrists and arms were too strong, and I had all the effectiveness of a gnat. I had never run so hard in my life. I was down seven-zip and getting desperate.

"Come on, Jane. Don't give up, Jane!" the newspaper people called.

Give up? Me?

In guys' lacrosse you can bodycheck; it's like football—you hurl your body at the guy with the ball and hope to knock him over and make him cough up the ball. Now Adam was moving toward the crease, looking for his ninth goal. I'd tried everything else, and maybe this would take him by surprise. I hurled with all my strength. Adam's body didn't move an inch, but mine went flying backward like a ball ricocheting off a brick wall. For a long moment I lay flat on my back, looking up at the sky. Every part of me ached.

Adam rushed over. His face peered down anxiously at mine. "What was that?"

"A body check."

"Are you *crazy?*"

"Maybe." I used my stick to get up. Mud now coated me back and front. I felt like a chocolate Easter bunny.

"Doing okay there, pal?" Josh asked me.

"Still breathing."

"I think we should stop," Adam said.

"Are you willing to forfeit?" I asked.

"She's a lunatic," he said to his friend.

But I wasn't. I'd stuck it out this long; I always finish what I start. And I wanted one goal, just one goal.

Think, think, think, I told myself. *What does Adam know now about how I play? What does he assume about me that I can use to my advantage?*

The next time I got the ball, I locked eyes with him. Marnie always used her eyes when she played, faking out others with her glances. Adam looked back at me, intent, curious, his eyes shining with the challenge.

For a moment I forgot what I was supposed to be doing. It was an odd feeling, like being suspended in time with him, like no one else was there with us. Then I blinked away the strange feeling and shifted my eyes to the right, focusing over his shoulder, trying to make him think I was driving in that direction as I usually did.

Just as I'd hoped, he overplayed me. I planted my foot and pivoted in the other direction, rolling off him in a perfect dodge. I had an open shot, the goal just ten feet away.

Quickly, like a reflex, his stick swung at me in a wraparound check.

Crack! He came down hard on my right forearm. It hurt so badly, I couldn't breathe. The ball shot loose and Adam rushed to pick it up.

"You okay?" he called back to me.

I nodded.

"Two-minute warning," someone hollered from the sidelines.

"Clear it," I croaked. My eyes smarted with tears, and I was glad to trail Adam up the field. Two minutes. I could hang in there for two more minutes.

Still, every time I checked him, my arm felt the vibration of our sticks as if it were being struck all over again. He scored another goal, and I knew I was down to my last chance. But I was also starting to see his moves better, to understand how they looked face-to-face on the field rather than from the stands. This time when I dodged, I kept my ball protected. The shot was long, but I took it, dropping the head of my stick, releasing the ball sidearm. Goal!

Cheers rang out. Even the guys' team was clapping. Adam grinned, a big, easy grin.

"Way to go!" he said, holding up his hand to give me a high five. For a moment our eyes held too, his sparkling with pleasure, making me sparkle inside.

We played a half minute more. When the timer yelled "game," the unglorious score was eleven to one. Adam removed his gloves to shake my hand. I kept on my right glove and tried not to wince.

The team and news staff and friends gathered

around us. Our sophomore photographer continued to take pictures. Adam removed his helmet. He was barely sweating, as if he'd been out for nothing more than a brisk walk. I was sweating like a pig and resembled one that had rolled in mud.

Not that it matters how I look, I told myself. I watched Kelly approach Adam, her notebook open and her pen poised to write, as if she were covering a real story.

I got a lot of pats on my back and thumps on my helmet, and surprisingly, many of them were from guys on the team.

Meanwhile Kelly was gazing up at Adam with large blue eyes, as if every word he uttered was fascinating. She kept tossing her head and laughing at what he said. Both of them were enjoying the conversation.

"Jane," Pablo said, "how come you never interview us the way she's interviewing Adam?"

"Yeah," said Billy. "I could get into that kind of questioning."

"I could get into that kind of answering," I countered, "instead of grouchy, three-word grunts."

Billy shook his head and laughed. "He's not answering—he's flirting. I've seen that look a million times before. It's how Adam handles girls."

So what does that make me? I wondered, and began to remove my equipment. "I'll clean this stuff up for you, Josh, and return it tomorrow."

"Nah, I'll take care of it," he said, taking the pads from me. "You go jump in a hot shower."

I glanced down at my throbbing arm, glad I had worn a long-sleeve T-shirt. "I need one. Thanks for reffing."

"You know, Jane," he said, "you make our team captain crazy."

"There's not much I can do about that, is there?" I replied.

Adam glanced up then, as if he sensed we were talking about him. There was a look of uncertainty on his face. Josh laughed quietly.

"What's funny?" I asked.

"He is. You are."

I shrugged and waved at Adam with my left hand. "If you still think we writers have it easy, let me know if you ever want to write a column," I called, then headed for the locker room.

I would never say writing was a piece of cake, but it sure left you feeling, and smelling, a lot better.

SEVEN

"WE'RE NOT GOING through your play-ground years again, are we?" Grandpa asked later that afternoon when I hobbled through the door with Marnie.

"Got any red bandages with stars on them?" I asked, then dropped down on a kitchen stool.

"Good thing the wedding isn't this week," Marnie told Grandpa. "She'd be one colorful maid of honor. We should probably get some ice on her right arm."

"Better yet, stuff me in the freezer," I suggested. I was starting to hurt all over.

Grandpa got out several plastic bags and filled them with ice. "What was the final score?" he asked.

"Marnie and company won fourteen to ten," I replied.

"And Jane made her point, one to eleven," Marnie added, grinning.

"We hope I did. Postgame tomorrow, when I start asking the guys questions, we'll see."

But as it turned out, Tuesday's away game wasn't a good test because Tilson won a solid victory. In fact, I'd never seen our offense and defense play so well. Naturally, the guys were happy to talk about the game. The most negative thing I could ask was why they hadn't played like this before. Adam's performance was outstanding. As the guys walked to the team bus, there was some quiet joking that I might have to prep him for the next game.

By Tuesday afternoon most of my sore muscles had disappeared, but I wore jeans and a long-sleeve cotton shirt that day and the next. I was mapped with bruises, and my right arm was a thing of wonder, black and blue and violet.

"I bet Daniel would find those colors inspiring," Marnie remarked when she took a peek at my arm on Wednesday.

That afternoon I was working late in the newspaper office with Tom and Kelly. At our staff meeting earlier we'd decided that if Kelly did a piece on Adam, she'd have to be fair and do features on the best athletes of every school sport. That was more work than she'd counted on, not to mention the fact that half of the candidates were girls and some of the guys were short and had acne. Kelly decided to withdraw the idea.

Now she sat two monitors down from me, struggling with another feature on the school cafeteria. As usual on deadline day, Tom was checking over the work that was already completed and on disk. That evening we'd send it over the Internet to a small commercial press. Our two thousand copies would be dropped off by lunch the next day.

My column was done, but I was struggling with Vinny's, trying to edit it so that it was still his work but actually said something interesting. I had my feet propped next to my computer, a pile of printouts on my lap, and was leaning back in my favorite chair, staring into space—a position that signaled to everyone who knew me that I was deep into my work and shouldn't be disturbed. I didn't hear Adam come in. When he tapped me on the shoulder, I jumped, sending a cascade of papers to the floor.

"Oh, sorry," he said, crouching down next to me to pick them up.

I never let guys pick up things I'm capable of retrieving myself, but this time I didn't move. Adam's sudden appearance made me feel strange—sort of disoriented. Usually I occupied his territory, but now he stood in the middle of mine, and everything in the office seemed to rearrange itself around him. Maybe I'd been plugged into my computer for too long.

"Do these papers go in some kind of order?" Adam asked, still in a crouch, his face a little lower than mine and looking up at me.

"No. Yes. I don't know. They're old drafts," I said, taking the pile from him.

"She gets like this when we're under deadline," Kelly told him.

He nodded at Kelly, then stood up and opened his gym bag, pulling a folder out of it. "I'll just leave this somewhere."

"Another letter to the editor?" Kelly asked, smiling at him with big, velvet eyes that made me think of pansies. I guess guys like that.

"Actually, it's an article." He turned back to me. "You said, whenever I wanted to write . . . I took you up on it."

"What's it on?" Tom asked from across the room.

"Basic lacrosse strategy," Adam said. "It's a guide for people who don't know the sport. I thought it might make it more interesting for the kids who aren't real fans but like to come to our games anyway. Is it something you could use?"

"Ask my sports editor," Tom replied.

"Sure," I said. "It's a good idea."

"I can edit it," Kelly offered, standing up and reaching for the folder he held. "Jane's a little behind."

"Kelly, it's too late for this week's edition," Tom pointed out. "Jane will edit it next week."

"Edit it?" Adam echoed.

I nodded. "I don't do much to articles by guest writers—check the grammar and accuracy of content, that's all."

"I know my stuff," he said.

"I just make sure you're saying what you mean to say."

"I'll scan it for you, Jane," Kelly said, "and put it into PageMaker. Adam can see how it looks in newspaper columns. Maybe he can suggest some photos from our files that would work with it."

"Is your feature done?" Tom asked her.

"I was just about to print out," she said.

Tom glanced at me. "It's up to you, Jane."

"Fine. Great," I said, and went back to work. Kelly was annoying me more than usual. And it bothered me that Adam's presence could break my concentration as easily as it had. We had visitors all the time; I'd never had trouble ignoring them.

I focused on the screen in front of me, reading Vinny's article for the millionth time. I twisted a piece of my hair till my finger was trapped. I untwisted it, then yanked on it. "Spit it out, Vinny," I muttered. "Spit it out!"

Adam burst out laughing, and I jumped again. He'd been standing behind me, reading over my shoulder.

"Sorry," he said, still grinning. "You sure do get intense."

"That's great coming from a guy who gets green fire in his eyes whenever he picks up a lacrosse stick."

Adam gazed down at me. There was a soft green light shining in them now.

I quickly turned back to my screen. "I think Kelly is ready for you."

"I am." She had pulled a chair close to hers. Adam sat down, and she showed him how to scan in the text, then convert it to our software. I went back to the impossible article on the girls' lacrosse team.

Some people on the newspaper say I'm overly conscientious and spend too much time on my work, but Grandpa had always said that the editor's job is not to write over, but to bring out the best in the voice of the writer. And that takes time—with Vinny, a lot of time.

I suddenly saw what I needed to do: By simply changing the order of three paragraphs, I could keep the paragraphs intact but show an interesting contrast. I pushed up my sleeves and went to work. "Yes, yes, yes," I said, watching the piece spring into shape.

"Cripe! Jane!" It was Adam again.

"What?" I muttered, admiring the way the article looked on my screen, congratulating myself for being an editorial genius. I felt him standing next to me. "You're determined to disrupt my work, aren't you?"

When he didn't reply, I looked up at him. He was staring at my arm. The bruise. I quickly pulled down both sleeves.

But he took my right arm in his hands and pushed up the sleeve slowly, carefully. There was a look of disbelief on his face.

"It's no big deal," I said.

He looked as if someone had just struck *him*. He cradled my arm with one hand and ran the fingers of his other hand softly over my skin.

"I remember when this happened. I checked you with a wraparound. Why didn't you say something? Why didn't you stop the game?"

I shrugged. "I finish what I start."

Still holding the badly bruised arm in one hand, he pushed up the sleeve on my other arm. I could hear him draw in his breath.

"It doesn't hurt," I said. Which was true—the last bit of pain had miraculously left, the way it did when I was five and Grandpa kissed my skinned knees. But unlike then, I felt a new and deeper ache, a hurting that went to the very center of me. I was aware of each place that Adam's fingers touched my arms. Could the gentleness with which another person held you actually make you ache?

"I bruise easily. Tell him, Tom," I said, wanting Adam to look somewhere other than at me. "Tell him," I repeated when Tom sat back in his chair with that thoughtful but inscrutable look he gets.

"All girls bruise easily," Tom said, winking at me.

I pulled my arms away from Adam and folded down my sleeves. "But Jane bruises more easily than you'd expect," Tom continued to Adam, his voice growing serious, "inside and out."

I reached for my mouse and clicked on print, glad for an excuse to walk to the other end of the room, where the printer was.

Adam sat down next to Kelly again. She read parts of his article aloud from the screen, praising it, and in fact, what I heard was very good.

I checked over my hard copy, then saved the file, but my mind was elsewhere. My verbal one-on-ones with Adam were safe when I was sure he was an egotistical jock who had trouble taking criticism. But now knowing how vulnerable he could be, how emotional he got about people he felt responsible for—his teammates and even me—*I* suddenly felt vulnerable too.

As soon as I handed my disk to Tom, I said good-bye to the three of them and fled.

"Stacy!" I exclaimed, surprised to see her as I walked my bike through the back-alley gate. She sat on our swing, a bench that hung from an A-frame. "What's up? Where's everyone?"

"Your mom's studying. Grandpa's starting dinner. They said you get home late on Wednesdays."

I put down my kickstand and pulled off my backpack, carrying it over to the swing. "You've been to the salon again," I observed. "New style." Her hair was pulled back sleekly against her head. "Turn around."

She did, showing me a tight bun coiled at the nape of her neck.

"Very sophisticated," I said, sitting down next to her. "Has Travis seen it?"

She nodded. "He loves it."

"And you?"

"Hate it."

"Then don't wear it. If Travis likes a bun, let him wear one."

She laughed. "You always make things seem so easy, Daisy. But they're not." She fingered a magazine that had a picture of a bride on the front of it.

"You must have a library of those by now," I said.

"The salon let me have it. They're awfully nice

to me."

"With the business you've been giving them lately, they can afford to buy you a subscription."

She rocked the swing with one foot. "While I was in my hairdresser's chair, I filled out this survey," she said, opening the magazine.

I leaned against her to see what it was. "'Are You Meant for Each Other?'" I read. There was a list of multiple-choice questions that continued onto the next page; some of the answers were circled in red ink, others in blue. "Which color is you?"

"Red," she replied. "Travis is blue."

"Travis filled this out?" I asked, surprised.

"No, I did it for him," she said. "He's entirely predictable. I had an easier time answering for him than for myself."

"Let's see." I skimmed the questions and answers.

If you unexpectedly inherited $10,000, you would
    (a) Invest it in the stock market
    (b) Put it in a savings account
    (c) Buy your mate an extravagant gift
    (d) Throw a party for all your friends

Stacy had circled (a) in blue—Travis would invest the money—and both (c) and (d) in red—gifts and parties were her choice. That seemed accurate to me. I found myself wondering for a moment what Adam would have circled, then quickly put that out of my mind.

While I was reading through the questions, Grandpa joined us. Stacy explained the survey to him, then pointed to a grid. "Here's how you figure out the score. The highest you can get is fifty, meaning a match made in heaven."

"What was your score?" I asked.

"Six."

"Oh." *Where was her match made?* I wondered.

"You know, Stacy, I've never put much stock in this kind of thing," Grandpa told her. "I don't mean you shouldn't be asking yourself questions. You need to pay attention to even the little conflicts and doubts you might have and decide if they mean something more. But I wouldn't worry about this."

"Maybe you should get Grandpa to fill out the survey," I suggested to Stacy. "Have him circle answers for him and Grandma, and see how they match up." I turned to him. "Mom said you guys were really different, that Grandma didn't like sports very much and you weren't big on the symphony."

"True enough," he replied, "but we enjoyed each other's differences." He stooped to pull a weed. "Besides, we had one sure sign we were meant for each other. At least, that's what your grandmother claimed."

"What was it?" Stacy and I asked at the same time.

"When I kissed her, her toes curled."

My cousin and I instinctively pulled our feet up on the swing and held our toes.

Grandpa laughed, threw the weed aside, then headed back to the kitchen.

"Okay, Daisy," Stacy said, giggling, "close your

eyes and imagine you're kissing someone."

"That's dumb," I said. "You do it."

"No, both of us," she urged.

"Why?"

"Come on, Dais. Please?"

I closed my eyes and imagined myself kissing Daniel. Then I grabbed my toes, making sure they were straight. But in the meantime the hands that so gently cupped my face and held it close had morphed into Adam's. With a start my eyelids flew open and I shook the image from my mind. I wasn't quite ready to know what my toes thought of Adam just yet.

EIGHT

AT LUNCHTIME ON Thursday, I was working through a pile of articles I was supposed to have read by my next class. "I should never have signed up for honors history," I said.

Marnie snuck a bite of her sandwich, keeping an eye out for Ms. Wong, our extrasensory librarian who could be back in the magazine stacks and still smell ham on rye. "That's what you get," Marnie replied, "for trying to schedule yourself out of Issues of Health & Conscience with Nurse Hatchet."

"Well, it worked, didn't it?" I grinned up at her. "Finally! Here comes Angela," I said, catching sight of our friend as she entered the library. "The paper should've been here an hour ago." Angela wove her way among the wooden tables.

"Hot off the press," she announced, dropping two copies of the paper between Marnie and me.

I reached for one. "Thanks, Ang—" I broke off,

startled by what I saw on the front page. "What's this?"

Marnie burst out laughing.

"Hardy and Logan Face-off," the headline said. The big, page-one photo showed Adam and me in a classic lacrosse shot, both of us wearing fierce expressions on our faces.

I stared at it. A funny picture of me covered with mud and looking crazed, hanging in the *Pipeline* office, was one thing; this was another. Marnie burst out laughing.

"More photos inside," the caption promised.

I quickly turned the page. An article recapping the match led off the sports page:

> Sticks cracked and mud flew as season-long rivals Hardy and Logan took the field Monday afternoon, each determined to annihilate the other—or at least shut each other up.

"Vinny didn't write this," I said. "Neither did Kelly."

"Ellen," Angela told me.

The sophomore who covered tennis for me—traitor!

"And Sam."

"Sam!" I exclaimed. He was the baseball reporter I had trained last year.

But I had to treat it like a joke. That's all it was, the staff having some fun. Marnie couldn't stop laughing, and I knew everybody in the school who followed sports would enjoy it.

I had gotten a hoot out of being a target in our April Fools' issue. So why did it feel so personal now?

I turned back to the first page. Did I really get that manic, determined look on my face? Is that what Adam saw?

"These papers were snapped up in the cafeteria," Angela told us.

"That's great." I forced a smile.

"Well, final delivery," Angela said, and headed over to Ms. Wong. I glanced up at the library clock, then silently rose to return my stack of books.

Marnie watched me. She had finally stopped laughing. "Jane?" she said when I returned and picked up my backpack. The bell rang. "I'll walk you to class."

"You don't need to."

Fortunately Marnie reads me well and knows when to ignore what I say. I was glad she was with me as we headed down the locker-lined hall.

"Great pics, Jane!" someone called.

"Thanks."

"When's the next match, Jane?"

"I'll let you know."

We turned the corner and headed down the stairway. I looked ahead and almost missed the next step. Adam and Josh were coming toward us. We met at the landing between the two flights of steps.

"Hi, guys," Marnie said.

"Hey, Marnie. Hey, Jane," Josh replied. The superfriendly sound in his voice warned me that all was not well.

So did Adam's eyes—they were the color of a stormy bay. But his voice was cool. "You pulled off quite a surprise, Jane."

"Do you mean the coverage of our match?"

"Are there any *other* surprises I should know about?" he asked tensely.

"Not that I can think of."

"Good," he replied, "because I'm in trouble enough with Coach."

"In trouble—for what?" People were jostling us from behind, trying to get around us on the stairway. "What are you talking about?" I asked.

"When Coach left practice early, we were supposed to gather the balls and leave too. You can't play on school property without a coach or teacher around. Everybody knows that. When we do it, we don't advertise."

I turned to Marnie, and she nodded. "It's the rule—because of insurance."

"The vice principal wasn't pleased," Adam went on.

"Well, nothing much pleases him," I remarked.

"He was in the athletic office when I got called in. Talked a lot about leadership, setting an example."

I got bumped hard from behind. The four of us pressed closer together.

"Look on the bright side," I said, "at least we know Mr. Yelton reads the paper and follows sports."

Adam's eyes shot sparks. "That's all you care about, isn't it—getting read!"

"Excuse me?"

"Getting noticed, making a splash," he said.

He was standing so close, I felt as if I had to put my head back to look at him.

"I thought things were better between us," he continued, "but in the end, you do whatever it takes to have people pay attention to you. You don't care about the consequences for anyone else."

"Get a grip," I replied, taking a step back and up so I'd be taller. "You are way overreacting. And let's be honest about who likes attention. Everybody does, but when you get it, you've got to take the good with the bad. I expect and accept criticism, the VP's or anyone else's. That's more than I can say for you."

"Yeah, well, at least I don't set people up," Adam replied angrily.

"What do you mean by that?" I challenged him.

"I think he means—," Josh began, trying to intervene.

"I mean I don't provoke people just to get a reaction I can print," Adam continued.

"You think that's what I do?"

"Maybe you should talk about this later," Josh suggested, "when you're both calmer."

"I don't play with people," Adam went on. "I don't fool with their feelings and use them to create a good story."

"And you think that's what I do?" I repeated, hurt and bewildered.

"Can you guys battle this out later?" Josh asked. "We're going to be late for class."

"No problem," I replied. "I've said all I have to say."

"That'll be the day," Adam said.

We brushed past each other. At the bottom of the steps I made a sharp left. Marnie turned right. "Where are you going?" she asked.

"To the VP's office to take the blame and make nicey-nice with Old Yeller. You'd better run or you're going to need a late slip," I told her, then hurried in the direction of the administrative offices.

"Jane, wait," she called after me. "Wait!"

I stopped and turned around.

"Why didn't you tell Adam you had nothing to do with the coverage?"

I didn't answer. I wasn't sure.

"Why didn't you let him know that you were as surprised as he was and not very happy about it?"

I played with my sleeve, pushing it up and down my bruised arm. He could get a rise out of me so easily. "What difference would it make?"

"Maybe a lot," Marnie replied. "The coach and vice-principal stuff is just stuff, just an excuse to vent. I think the problem is that Adam's taken this incident personally."

"He takes everything personally," I told her.

"Everything related to you," she pointed out, then hurried to her next class.

Mr. Yelton was his old reliable self. He lectured me for several minutes, then told me to keep up the good work with the paper and sent me on my way with a late note that did not require detention.

The rest of the day I got a lot of teasing, and I wondered what Adam was getting on his end. I wondered, too, what Mr. Clarke would say if he saw this week's edition.

Fortunately the girls' lacrosse team played that day, as did the guys' baseball team. There was a tennis match too, so I kept busy after school running from place to place, talking to my reporters and avoiding guys' lacrosse.

When I arrived home late that afternoon, Grandpa was cooking and Mom was studying as usual.

"Stacy called," Grandpa told me. "Something about getting the maid-of-honor dress fitted tomorrow. You need to call her back. Where's my paper?" he asked.

"It's coming," I said, unzipping my backpack.

"You've got E-mail, hon," Mom called from the dining room.

I handed Grandpa the paper, then sat down next to Mom to retrieve the mail. I heard Grandpa explode with laughter.

"Can you keep it down in there?" I fussed.

"Nice photo, Daisy Jane! I want a print of it autographed by you and Adam. I'll hang it next to my Cal Ripken and Johnny Unitas."

"Wait till you see the pictures inside," I muttered, then clicked open my mail.

Another burst of laughter drew my mother out of her chair. She stood next to Grandpa and read. She started laughing too. "That's my little girl," she said, "all sugar and spice."

"Yeah, yeah," I replied, clicking the mouse again. Daniel's letter came up on my screen.

Dear Jane,

Doing this fast—waiting for plaster to dry. My 3-Ds are awesome these days; wish you could see them. You gave me the dates of the wedding and spring dance too early, so I forgot to write them down. Sorry I can't come. Said yes to other things. I hope this doesn't mess you up too much.

Daniel

"Men are scum," I said aloud.

Grandpa and Mom looked up from the paper.

"Does that include old men?" Grandpa asked.

"Bad news?" my mother said, coming to stand behind me and laying her hand on my shoulder. "May I read?"

"Sure."

She scanned the note on the screen, then remarked gently, "He didn't give you much warning."

"I don't need a date to go to the dance," I told her, "and I don't need an escort for the wedding. I'll go and have a good time anyway. But Daniel's attitude is starting to get to me. He's thoughtless. He's . . . careless with other people."

"He's young," Mom replied, touching my cheek lightly. "Though I realize my saying that doesn't make you feel any better."

"This is what will make me feel better," I said, and clicked Daniel into oblivion.

NINE

I HAD TO cover the guys' lacrosse match on Friday afternoon, so Stacy made the appointment with the seamstress late that day and said she'd pick me up from the game.

"Why don't you come early?" I suggested. "Adam will be playing."

Stacy had never been big on sports, so I didn't think she'd attend the game. But I hoped she'd mention it to Travis or Adam's mother and somebody from home would find a little time. Why it mattered to me that Adam got family support, especially after the obnoxious things he'd said on the stairway—well, that was something I didn't want to think about.

The next afternoon Stacy surprised me, showing up during halftime. I'd just finished a quick interview with Grizzly and was sitting in the stands directly behind our team bench. Vinny was sitting behind the opponent's bench with instructions to concentrate on the other team's play. Even if this strategy didn't produce more focused writing, it would at least keep him from thumping on my back. Kelly and Angela sat with me, and it was Kelly who pointed out Stacy walking along the sidelines.

"Who's that girl?" she said.

"You mean the one who just blew in?" Angela asked, smiling.

It was one of those breezy spring days when tree blossoms streamed down like pink and white confetti. The wind made Stacy's red hair wild and her short skirt almost impossible to hold down. She walked along the sidelines, searching for me, unaware of the fact that spectators weren't supposed to be meandering through the players when they were prepping for play. The guys on our team watched her with curious expressions on their faces. I waved to get her attention and get her off the field.

"Hi, Daisy!" she called out brightly.

Adam, who was talking to Coach, turned around quickly.

"Excuse me," she said, stepping up on the bleachers in the small space between Pablo and Josh so she could sit next to me. They looked at each other and grinned. Adam rubbed the back of his neck and turned back to his conference with Coach.

I introduced my cousin to Angela and Kelly and, of course, had to explain the Daisy thing. Stacy settled down on the bleacher seat and scanned the players.

"Which one is Adam?" she asked. "They all look alike in their hats."

"Helmets," Kelly corrected her sweetly.

"In the white jersey, number twenty-four," I said, pointing as the guys took the field. "His friend, Josh, is number fifteen."

Stacy stood up. "Go, Adam!" she hollered. "Show 'em how it's done!"

Several guys on the bench turned around to look at her.

"Not that I know how it's done," she said, plopping down next to me.

"You'll catch on," Kelly replied.

I sure hoped so because as delicate as Stacy looked, she could project her voice like a foghorn.

The guys strode to their starting positions, with Grizzly shouting last-minute instructions and encouragement. The two face-off men bent over their sticks. The ref placed the ball between them and backed off, and the second half began. We lost the face-off but alertly intercepted a pass and brought the ball upfield. Angela filled Stacy in on the basic rules of the game while I scribbled down notes.

"Hey!" Stacy cried out as Adam cradled the ball and a defenseman tried to check him. "That's no fair! He's got a longer pole. Why, he could take that thing crabbing!"

I explained to her that the various positions used different equipment.

She was quiet for a minute. "That boy's hitting Adam. Foul!" Stacy cried out, jumping to her feet. "Foul, ump! Call it!"

Grizzly glanced over his shoulder at us. Angela

looked at me, her dark eyes dancing with laughter.

Although Stacy was protective of Adam on the offense, she eventually became adjusted to the roughness of the game, and as the score seesawed back and forth, she grew bloodthirsty when we were on defense.

"Kill 'em!" she shouted at Adam as he checked a guy. "Shove it down his throat!"

She kept the game chatter going into the fourth quarter. "Zing it in there! Make him eat it!"

Out of the corner of my eye I could see some of the guys on the bench, laughing.

With three minutes to go and a tie game, the rest of the crowd was getting whipped up. Coach, who'd been hollering through all four quarters, went into his final-minutes frenzy, crouching down, leaping up, covering his head, waving his arms.

"Would you look at him!" Stacy said, laughing, as if she had been sitting perfectly quiet. "It's like he's playing in the game himself."

"He is," I said. "That's Grizzly, our head coach."

"Grizzly, as in bear?" she asked.

"His last name is Gryczgowski," I explained.

"Jeez, that's worse than Olstenheimer."

"Come on, sharp passes!" Marnie called.

"Why'd he do that?" Stacy asked.

I thought she meant our crease attackman. "Because he was losing his cool and trying to do it all himself. We need to look for our cutters and be more patient."

"No, I mean why did your coach just throw a glass of water in his own face?"

"Same reason," I told her. *Thataway,* I silently cheered on Adam as he cut through the middle and quick-sticked the incoming pass.

"Goal!" shouted Angela and Kelly. The guys on the sideline jumped up and down. Those on the field punched the air with their fists. Pablo thumped Adam on the back.

"Adam just scored a goal," I said to Stacy. "We're one up."

"Bear is hugging everybody."

"You mean Grizzly," I told her.

The players set up for a face-off. "Come on, hold them now!" Angela was yelling. "Hold them."

"Thirty seconds!" Coach hollered at the guys, running a hand through his thick, curly brown hair. "Thirty seconds! . . . Twenty-five . . . twenty . . ."

Stacy was counting down with him.

The other team passed the ball quickly. Their middy set a screen.

"Josh!" hollered Coach.

Josh blocked the shot with his foot, but another player scooped it up and passed it out to a cutter, who fired a second bullet. Josh dove, skidding on his stomach, and stopped the ball. The whistle blew. We'd won!

"Catch up with you in a bit, Stacy," I said, then jumped down to the field to begin interviews.

They went well. Our performance hadn't been sterling through all four quarters, and the guys were honest about it. Josh, as always, gave me the most useful quotes. He leaned on me comfortably, his forearm on my shoulder as if I were a shelf while we talked and I jotted notes. When I looked up, I saw Adam about fifteen feet down the sideline, staring at us. Josh saw him too, and I heard him laugh quietly.

"What's funny?" I asked Josh. "And don't say, 'He is, you are.'"

Josh grinned down at me without answering and moved on.

I headed toward Adam, but Kelly got to him just before I did. There was no point in trying to have a conversation as long as she was there to give a positive spin to each of our statements, making sure Adam knew how much she admired him. I continued on toward Coach, but Adam caught me by the arm.

He quickly let go of it—maybe he remembered it was the bruised one—and pulled me back by my shirt.

"Why is Stacy here?" he asked.

"I invited her."

He studied me for a moment, his face full of curiosity. I had the feeling he was pleased she had come but would never admit it. "Why did you ask her? She doesn't like sports. She doesn't know anything about them."

"She knows you," I replied. "Congrats on the win. I'll catch you later for some questions, okay?" I glanced at Kelly, then continued on toward Grizzly.

"Hey, Coach."

"Hi, Jane." He smiled at me with warm brown eyes. His dark, curly hair was still wet from one of the guys pouring a victory cup of ice over his head. "What would you like to know?"

"Well, I could use some general comments about the game and how it fits in with the rest of the season, then I have a few specific questions."

"Okeydoke."

As we talked, I didn't notice that Stacy had come to stand next to me—but Coach did.

"Coach," I said when I saw him looking at her, "this is Stacy, my cousin. And Adam's future sister-in-law."

Coach smiled and shook her hand.

"Nice to meet you, Grizzly," Stacy said.

Coach's eyebrows jumped up, then his smile showed in his eyes too.

"We don't call him Grizzly to his face," I told Stacy.

"Oops."

"But—but you can," Coach said.

She touched him on the wrist. "Thank you, Grizzly. It's been real fun to be here."

"Thanks for coming to watch Adam," he replied quietly. "I've been hoping some of his family would get here. He's a fantastic player and a great kid. It's a shame for them to miss his games."

"It is a shame," she agreed.

There was a long silence. It was as if they wanted to talk to each other but could think of nothing else to say.

I waited a moment more, then started questioning Coach again. He answered me, but as he talked, he kept looking at Stacy as if she, too, were interested in the fine points of the game—which was a hoot. Then I glanced sideways: She did look fascinated!

The guys headed back to the locker room, but Coach was still talking. I had never gotten so many quotes from him before. The three of us walked slowly off the field and toward the bridge that connected the upper and lower athletic fields. Adam was waiting there for us.

"Thanks for coming, Stacy," he said when she saw him. "It was a nice surprise."

"You were wonderful, wonderful!" my cousin told him, climbing the two steps onto the bridge to give him a big hug. He smiled and hugged her back, his muscular arms reaching around her.

I stared at Adam's arms and strong hands, remembering how they'd looked when he'd carefully held mine. Stacy was about the same size as I, and I looked at how she measured up against him, how her shoulder fitted in under his where her face touched his jersey.

I made myself glance away, then saw that Coach was watching them with just as much interest. I had a bad feeling that he wasn't thinking, "With arms like that, we should work more on Adam's wraparound check." Coach probably wasn't thinking about Adam at all, but noticing how Stacy looked in the arms of a guy the same height and build as he.

Could someone fall for another person that fast? I wondered. *Worse—have I fallen for a guy I thought I'd never get along with?*

The four of us started walking again, Coach with Stacy, Adam with me. I focused on my notepad, asking Adam questions, scribbling answers, trying not to lose my place. He accidentally brushed against me. Twice. I wished he'd brush against me again.

It's this weather, I told myself. *It's this soft, April air doing strange things to us all.*

Who knew what would happen when May came.

"Could you turn the air conditioner on?" I asked Stacy as soon as we got in the car.

"I'm feeling kind of warm myself," she said, flicking the switch.

Neither of us spoke on the way to the bridal salon.

Gianelli's was the fanciest shop I'd ever been in, with silk-covered chairs scattered about, little sofas in the dressing rooms, and a ladies' room offering dishes of soap carved like roses.

The seamstress, who had altered Stacy's gown, hung it and the veil in the dressing room set aside for us. Stacy tried them on, and I stood there with my mouth open.

"You look . . . unbelievably beautiful," I said. It was the truth, and my saying it immediately brought tears to Stacy's eyes.

"Cut it out," I told her. "You know you're the one person who can get me blubbering."

She smiled and wiped her eyes.

The seamstress, a woman with short, gray hair and big owl glasses, looked Stacy over like a painting

90

she'd just finished. "Perfect," she said. "All we need is a little pressing now." Then she helped Stacy out of her dress and got me into mine, a sophisticated violet silk sheath.

"Daisy! What have you done to yourself?" Stacy exclaimed, noticing my bruises.

"I'll be a normal color in two weeks," I assured her.

"Please take care of yourself. Remember your first ballet recital," she warned.

My first and last. The day before I was to put on the sequined tutu, I'd tried to ride my tricycle down five cement steps. I'd made it to the recital, but as I'd skipped and twirled, adhesive bandages kept flying off.

"Don't worry," I told her. "I've got a better bike."

The seamstress began to pull and pin. As the woman worked on the dress, Stacy sat on the love seat, looking at me and glowing. "I'm going to make a prediction, Daisy. All the unattached guys at the wedding are going to take one look and fall madly in love with you."

"Like who?" I asked. "Travis's great-uncle with the portable TV?"

"You know," she went on, "I wanted my bridesmaids to wear pink. Long, pink gowns."

"You've wanted that since you were eight."

She nodded. "Travis wouldn't allow it."

"Let me guess. He thought pink would clash with your hair."

"Now I see that Travis was right. The violet looks wonderful on you."

"How could he be right?" I argued. "He didn't know I was going to be the maid of honor when he told you what to do."

The seamstress glanced up at me, raising one eyebrow, then went back to her work.

"Wait till Adam sees you," Stacy went on. "He'll think the violet is perfect for you."

I'd been trying not to think about what Adam might think because I didn't want it to matter to me. When a guy's view matters, you start doing things you never would've done before.

"How come Adam's family doesn't come to watch him play?" I asked.

"Well, they're very busy people," Stacy said, leaning back against the love seat, watching me in the mirror. "They have a lot of business affairs to attend, charity events, political fund-raisers, the symphony, the theater—they're always going somewhere."

"If they have time for all that, they have time to go to one game," I told her. The intensity of my own voice surprised me. "I mean, Adam seemed really glad to have you there," I added lightly.

"I suppose I could mention it to his mother," Stacy said, then opened her bag and pulled out a nail file. Her nails didn't need any work; they were being manicured several times a week now so they'd be in perfect shape for the wedding. But Stacy always fooled with her nails when something bothered her.

"Adam and his stepfather don't get along very well," she said. "Mr. Clarke kind of calls the shots in that house."

The same way Travis will when you and he set up house, I thought.

"He wanted Adam to go to Gilman School, where both he and Travis went," Stacy continued. "Of course, Mr. Clarke was going to pay for it. But Adam refused the offer, which didn't go over well."

"Why did Adam refuse?" I asked. Gilman was the most prestigious school in Baltimore, an all-guys school with a gorgeous campus and strong academics—not to mention a super lacrosse team.

"I don't know," Stacy replied, then sawed away at a nail. "Except sometimes, I feel like saying *no* too."

"Do you?"

"I always get over it," she said, then put the file away. "Daisy, you look so beautiful!"

I studied myself in the mirror. The seamstress was working a miracle.

"Pretty amazing," I replied, and despite my resolution not to, thought about what Adam might say when he walked me down the aisle in this dream of a dress.

TEN

MARNIE CAME OVER on Saturday morning just to hang out. We shot baskets in the back alley and talked about next week's dance, to which neither of us had a date.

"What exactly happened with Daniel?" she asked.

"I already told you. I sent him to electronic oblivion."

"You didn't tell me why."

I took my favorite shot from the alley speed bump. "It seems he forgot to write the dance and wedding on his calendar. Now he has other plans."

"He sure has a way of forgetting whatever someone's counting on him to do."

"I know," I said, passing the rebound to her. "The thing is, I saw how he was with the little kids at camp. Half the time he was so caught up in his own stuff, he didn't pay attention to them. I don't know why I thought he'd be different with me."

Marnie took a jump shot from the edge of a large pothole. *Swish, bang*—through the basket and off the trash can. "Love is blind," Marnie said, opening the gate to Mrs. Bean's yard to retrieve the ball.

"It wasn't love. It was—" I shrugged.

"Convenience?" she suggested.

"Living in two different cities is not convenient."

"Unless you like distance," Marnie observed, and tossed the ball out to me. "Unless you feel a little safer with distance between you."

"What do you mean?"

"With forty-something miles between the two of you *and* with Daniel's way of doing things, there's no chance of you relying on him, is there?"

I didn't answer, just bounced the ball steady and low to the ground, scattering pebbles.

"Jane," she said, "you know how you dislike it when someone helps you. You know how being dependent on another person scares you. Well, there's no chance of that with Daniel. He's totally unreliable."

I nodded and continued to dribble the ball, as if I were trying to bore a hole in the concrete. "Sometimes I wish you didn't know me so well."

"But I do, and I'm your best friend anyway," she said, then laughed and swiped the ball from me.

We played a sloppy one-on-one, and once again the ball landed in Mrs. Bean's yard. We raced each other through the gate, pushing and shoving and laughing. I got to the ball first, and Marnie tried to wrench it out of my hands.

"Jump ball," called a deep voice. We looked up. Coach was standing on the back porch. At least, a version of Coach.

He hadn't shaved yet, and the dark curls on one side of his head—probably the side he'd slept on—were flattened and pushed in funny directions. His jeans, which were far tighter than anything he wore to PE class, had holes in them, and his sweat-shirt was frayed around the neck and sleeves. He came down the steps, holding on to his coffee mug like it was a life-support system, being trailed by his overweight cat.

"Hey, Big Mama," I greeted the cat.

"Is this the kitty you trapped in the bureau drawer?" Marnie asked as we knelt down to pet her.

Coach nodded, then crouched down next to us. "Here's where she likes to be scratched," he said, running his fingers very gently around the back of the cat's ears. "And under the chin—don't you, baby," he murmured.

Big Mama flopped over on her side.

"Oh, yeah, you like that," Coach said, his voice tender. "You like that sweet ol' belly rubbed."

Marnie glanced sideways at me, sucking in her lips, trying not to laugh. I wondered if Coach had selected the heart-shaped ID tag that dangled from the cat's pink collar.

We let Big Mama smell us, then petted her tummy and chin as she stretched back luxuriously on the warm concrete. Coach stood up. "You have new buddies," he said to his cat, sounding pleased, then headed toward Mrs. Bean's garage, emerging from there a few minutes later with a rake and a bag of grass seed.

"Need some help?" I asked.

"Thanks, but no thanks," he said. "This is part of the apartment deal—I pay almost nothing for rent. Besides, I enjoy it."

As he started to rake, the cat leaped to its feet and hopped up on the picket fence to watch. "My supervisor," he told us with a smile, then went back to work, whistling softly to himself.

Marnie and I returned to the alley and played a round of horse. We had just started a second game when a car turned down the alley. The driver was swerving left and right, desperately trying to avoid the potholes. I didn't know who it was—no one on our alley owned a Mercedes, and the reflection of trees and sky on the tinted glass kept us from seeing who was inside. Marnie and I quickly moved over to the fence, but the driver stopped and parked the car in the center of the alley. A door opened.

"Travis!" I exclaimed.

"Watch the doors. Don't bang them against the fence," he said as Stacy and Adam got out from the other side.

"Hey, Daisy," Stacy called cheerfully. "We just picked up your shoes for the wedding and decided to drop them by."

"Not one of our better ideas," Travis remarked. "There are no parking spaces on your street. There are none in this neighborhood."

"It's Saturday, and everyone's home," I explained. "Travis, this is my friend Marnie."

"Nice to meet you," Marnie told him. "Hey, Adam."

"Hi, Marnie. Jane," Adam said, coming toward us. He handed me a box of shoes. "I'm glad I'm not the one who's got to hobble around on these."

"Daisy, I found the most fantastic purse for you," Stacy said. "Wait till you see it!"

"Watch the doors," Travis reminded her again.

She pulled several shopping bags out of the car and began sorting through them.

"Hey, Coach," Adam called.

Coach waved but kept his distance.

Stacy's head suddenly popped up. "Hi, Grizzly," she said, looking surprised to see him. "I didn't know you lived here."

"Just moved in."

Adam introduced his stepbrother to Coach, who came over to the fence, still holding on to his rake, and shook Travis's hand. "Congratulations. Best wishes for the big day."

Travis nodded and glanced up at Mrs. Bean's place. "Nice house," he said. "Not much to keep up."

"Actually, I just rent the third floor," Coach explained.

"Oh."

"Which really *isn't* much to keep up," Coach said, smiling.

"Here it is, Daisy," Stacy said, removing the lid from a store box. "The purse to die for. What do you think?"

"Uh, well . . ." I thought it looked just like Stacy. It was violet satin, the same shade as my dress, about six inches wide and shaped like a heart. A huge, violet satin rose was sewn in the center of the heart, and silver, sequined leaves sprouted out from it. A braided rope with tassels was attached to the heart's exaggerated humps, so I could hang the purse on my shoulder.

"It's great," I lied, removing it from its box to show Marnie. It was the last purse in the world I would've chosen. But it was Stacy's wedding; I'd carry it if she wanted me to. "Thanks! Thanks a lot."

I caught Adam looking at me, a glint of amusement in his eyes.

"Stacy," Travis said, taking the purse from my hands, "this is the tackiest thing I've ever seen."

Everyone turned to him.

"What do you mean?" Stacy asked, sounding hurt.

"Just what I said," he replied. "It's like that pink, heart-shaped pillow with layers of lace you picked out for the ring bearer. It's like the blue-and-pink flower arrangements you suggested for the head table."

"Blue and pink flowers grow together in gardens all the time," Stacy argued.

"It's like the little flowered wallpaper you picked out for the downstairs bathroom. Tacky."

"The wallpaper may be old-fashioned," Stacy admitted, "but it's pretty. You know I'm the sentimental type."

"Sentimental is one thing; tasteless is another."

I felt like kicking him. I could see Adam's hand tense, the way it did when my questions angered him.

Coach stared at Travis for a long moment, then said, "Well, I've got a lot of work to do," and headed for the other side of the yard.

"Good thing," Marnie whispered to me from behind. "Travis would look terrible with a rake in his back."

"There's no such thing as tasteless, Travis," Stacy told him. "There are simply a lot of different tastes."

"Well, yours is certainly different, different than the taste of most of my friends who will be attending the wedding," he said.

I'd had enough. "Do you want to use that?" I asked Travis, pointing to the purse.

"Definitely not."

"Good," I replied, taking it back from him, "then I can. Stacy, I'll put this inside with the shoes. Thanks for dropping them by."

I headed toward the house with both boxes, and Marnie silently followed me.

"Jane," Adam called after me. "Wait up."

I kept walking.

"I want to talk to you," he said.

"I've just been put in a real bad mood," I warned him as I reached the steps of our back porch.

"Like I've only seen you in a good one?"

I spun around.

He grinned. It was a totally disarming smile. I took a step back and up.

100

"One more step," he said, laughing softly, "and you can be taller than me."

I guessed he'd noticed my tactic when he'd blown up at me on the school stairs. I stepped down to pavement level. "It'll be easier to kick you in the shin from here."

That sunlit smile again. The light in his eyes was making it hard for me to act huffy. Then his face grew serious. "Listen, what I wanted to tell you was that I'm sorry about acting like a jerk Thursday. I jumped the gun on you, thinking you knew what the rest of the staff had done, even thinking you had set me up for it."

I glanced sideways at Marnie. "Who told you?"

"Kelly. I feel really bad about it. Even if you had been part of the joke," he continued, "I should've had more of a sense of humor. I'm sorry about what I said. Lately it seems like—I don't know—like I've been taking everything way too seriously."

I saw Stacy and Travis getting into the car with grim expressions on their faces. I wondered if Travis ever said he was sorry.

"It's hard not to take stuff seriously," I said, "when other people are expecting big things from you. Even more, when you're expecting a lot from yourself."

I saw the surprise on Adam's face, as if he couldn't imagine that I would know how he felt. His green eyes wouldn't let mine go.

"So, uh, what kind of purse will *you* be carrying?" I asked, before I became totally mesmerized.

"Something in black satin with leather roses."

I laughed.

"Adam!" Travis hollered from the car.

"Coming." To Marnie and me he said, "Next time I help them with errands, I'm bringing a referee's whistle." He jogged down the path and through our gate.

Marnie leaned against the stair railing, a coy look on her face. "I wonder if Adam's got a date for the dance," she mused.

"Why? Are you planning to ask him?"

"I wonder if he's got a date to the wedding," she went on.

"Kelly would know," I said as I climbed the steps to the back door. "She knows everything."

Marnie caught up with me. "Why don't you ask him? To the dance, I mean."

"Yeah, right."

"And then to the wedding," she said.

"Marnie, be real."

"Give me a good reason why you shouldn't," she insisted.

"Because we're just—just—"

"Friends?"

I pulled open the door. "More like the best of enemies."

"Oh. Then what have you got to lose?"

ELEVEN

SUNDAY AFTERNOON MOM and I sprawled out in plastic lawn chairs in the backyard, both of us wearing our comfy old jeans, studying. Well, she was studying; I was making up for lost sleep. When the cordless phone rang, I nearly capsized.

Mom picked up the phone. "Hello . . . Stacy?" she said. "Stacy, slow down. What? Slow down, hon. Take a deep breath. Yes, Daisy's right here." Mom handed me the phone, holding her hand over the mouthpiece. "I can't make head or tail of what she's saying."

"Hi, Stacy."

"Daisy," she gasped into the phone, "you've got to help me. My ring is in the garden. They have tulips, hyacinths, all these azaleas and paths, I don't know what to do, I don't know why they have to plant so many darn pansies."

"Back up," I said to Stacy. "Whose garden? Where?"

"I don't know *where,*" she wailed. "Somewhere behind the Clarkes' house."

"What ring—not your diamond?"

"Travis is going to *kill* me," Stacy said.

I didn't like Travis, but I would've killed her too. The engagement ring was a two-karat diamond surrounded by sapphires.

"We were having brunch with his parents out in the garden and had a fight about the reception music. Travis had made up a list that I was to take to the bandleader last week, but on the way I, uh, added a few songs."

"A few sentimental songs?"

"Yes. I told him during brunch, and we started fighting. He doesn't know, but afterward I took the ring off and threw it."

"Oh, boy."

"Meet me there, okay? Please?" she begged. "Travis is going to be working all afternoon at his apartment. Mr. and Mrs. Clarke are at a party at somebody's skybox. I've got to find it, Daisy!" She gave me the address, and I hung up. I quickly explained things to Mom, who offered me her car. Ten minutes later I drove down the Clarkes' street just behind Stacy and followed her red Saturn to the house.

The Clarkes lived in an old neighborhood, where huge homes were built years before the city had actually reached its limits. Their house was a stone-and-stucco structure, very English looking with its gables and double chimneys. We parked in front of it and met in the driveway.

"You're sure no one's here," I said, looking up at the windows.

"Positive."

"You didn't mention Adam."

"He's out. Mr. Clarke was fuming because Adam had other plans today and wouldn't go with them to the skybox," she explained, then led me through a gate in a long hedge.

"Jeez!" I said when I saw how much property lay behind the house. The garden had a cluster of huge old lilac bushes with a bench set among them, beds of spring flowers, one whole section of topiary, and what appeared to be azaleas planted in a maze. "They could give tours of this place. So, where did you throw it?"

"I'm not sure."

"You must have some idea," I told her.

"Daisy, you know I've never had good aim. Besides, I wasn't aiming at anything."

"Well, where did it look like it dropped?"

"I don't know," she replied. "I didn't want to know, so I shut my eyes."

"Stacy!"

She blinked hard. Tears would only make things worse.

"Okay, okay. Let's think. Where were you standing when you threw it?"

She looked around, then walked past the lilacs to an old-fashioned sundial surrounded by pansies.

I picked up a pebble roughly the size of a ring and handed it to her. "Throw it."

She did, and I watched where it landed.

I picked up several more stones from the garden path. "Try it a couple of times so we can get a range."

We got a range, all right. One pebble landed about twenty feet to the right of the first. The next one landed fifteen feet to the left. Another stone carried only ten feet in front of us.

"Do you remember if you threw it overhanded or under?" I asked, noting she had made different kinds of tosses.

She flexed the fingers of her right hand and ran her tongue over her lips. "No."

I handed her another stone. "You're angry, Stacy, really angry. Think about how you felt and throw it."

She did.

"Well, that narrows it down," I observed bleakly. I had no idea she could hurl something that far. We'd be here all afternoon. "I wonder where we could get one of those metal detectors."

"The ring will glitter," she replied. "We'll see it."

"Why don't we check the yellow pages?" I continued.

"Let's just look for it first."

"They must sell those machines somewhere."

"Please, Daisy," she pleaded, her voice shaking. "I need to find it *now*."

"Okay, okay."

We wasted the next fifteen minutes wandering around, hoping the diamond would flash in the sun and catch our attention. At last I said, "Listen, Stacy, we're going to have to do this more methodically.

We'll start with the most likely area and work our way across it side by side in a straight line."

She nodded silently.

"Come on, kneel down next to me," I told her as I got down on the ground. I saw her stiffen her jaw so her chin wouldn't quiver. "We'll find it—promise," I said, patting the grass next to me.

She knelt beside me, and we moved forward slowly on our hands and knees, working our way through the flower bed, leaving a path of mashed pansies behind us. When we had gone as far as I thought Stacy could throw, I grabbed some garden stakes to mark the spot, then we shifted over a foot and started crawling back in the opposite direction. Our fingers pulled and poked and felt their way through the flowers.

We were halfway down the second row when we heard the approach of a car out front. Stacy and I froze. The car sounded as if it had turned into the Clarkes' driveway.

"What do we do?" Stacy whispered.

"Get down. Stay low." We flattened ourselves like lizards. "Maybe it's just somebody turning around."

The car motor idled. It couldn't have been more than thirty yards away, but the hedge barred us from seeing the driveway. I lifted myself up a little.

"It's a black car; I can just see the top."

"Mr. Clarke has a black Lincoln!" Stacy said in a panicky voice.

The driver turned off the engine, and we heard two car doors open and close.

"Come on, this way," I whispered. "Stay down! Stay down!"

We crawled as fast as we could toward the azalea maze. The bushes would hide us better than the tulips and pansies, and there was a garden shed just past its winding paths if we could make it that far. Sharp stones pressed into our hands and knees as we hurried along. I heard Stacy stifle a cry. At last we were on the soft grass paths among the azaleas.

I stopped. "We'll stay here," I whispered, "until we hear them go inside."

"What if they decide to stroll through the garden? Mrs. Clarke loves her garden."

"Hush."

We waited. And waited. I thought I heard footsteps on the driveway, but there was still no sound of someone entering the house. Long minutes ticked by. We must have crawled through a ton of pollen: Stacy kept rubbing her nose, and I was sucking down sneezes.

Maybe they had gone around to the other side of the house. With my hands I parted the branches of a bush, then wedged my head in as far as I could, trying to peer through it and see if someone was nearby.

"What are you doing, Jane?"

I jumped about a foot, my head still in the bush, then pulled out of it and spun around.

Adam was watching us from behind, standing on the other side of a wall of orange azalea, his hands on his hips, his head tilted to one side. Coach stood next to him with a look of curiosity on his face.

"Weeding. Would you like to help?"

I rose with Stacy and dusted off my knees. The last time we had looked this guilty, we'd put on globs of her mother's makeup, then ran into Aunt Susan at the 7-Eleven.

"We were looking for something," I said. "Actually, we were looking for Stacy's engagement ring."

Adam's eyes opened wide. "You mean the rock?"

I nodded and glanced sideways at Stacy. She was terribly embarrassed. I knew from the way her mouth pursed that it wouldn't take much to make her cry.

"She and Travis had a fight about the reception music," I said quietly. "He doesn't know, but she got mad and threw it."

Adam started to laugh but was stopped by Grizzly, who correctly read the look on my cousin's face. "Are you all right, Stacy?" Coach asked.

One tear spilled down her face, making her mascara run.

"Don't worry. We'll find it," he assured her, his voice as soft as it was when he talked to Big Mama. He dug tissues out of the pockets of his windbreaker and handed them across the bushes to Stacy. Coach pointed on his face to the position of the long streak of black that ran down from one of Stacy's eyes. She tried unsuccessfully to wipe it away, then Grizzly stretched over the bushes, took the tissue from her, and gently wiped her cheek.

"With four of us hunting we're sure to find it, Stacy," Adam said. He glanced past me. "Looks as if you've already searched the pansies."

So he had noticed our trail. Even before that, he'd probably noticed Stacy's car.

"I saw the Saturn parked out front," he said, as if reading my mind.

"So I guess you weren't worried about intruders," I replied, a bit miffed. "Thanks for sneaking up on us."

"Easy, Jane," he said lightly. "You would've done the same thing if you'd seen Coach and me racing across the garden on our hands and knees, trying to keep low."

"You saw that?" I could feel the color rising in my cheeks.

He grinned. "So, where should we start?"

The four of us walked back to the plot of garden where Stacy and I had been searching. My cousin and I got down on our knees again, this time with Coach on her right side and Adam on my left. We crawled at a slow pace, our fingers working carefully, trying to harvest a diamond.

"Adam and I went to the new lacrosse museum today," Coach said as we moved along.

"At Homewood?" I asked.

"Yeah," Adam replied. "While we were there, we got to watch the Johns Hopkins team practice. I would do anything to work out with a college team."

My fingers felt something small and round. They closed around it eagerly, then I tossed aside a stone. "Maybe I shouldn't ask this, Adam—"

"When has that stopped you?"

"Once, maybe," I told him. "Why didn't you go

to Gilman? The recruiters from Hopkins and other colleges are sure to check out that team. And Stacy said Mr. Clarke offered to pay the tuition."

Adam was quiet for a moment. "Same reason you don't tell people you're Jimmy Olsten's grandkid," he said. "I want to earn my own way."

"So you can do things the way *you* want to do them, without worrying about pleasing or owing someone else?"

Adam turned his head toward me. "It's scary the way we think the same."

"About some things, yes."

We continued on in silence. The sun felt warm on my back, and the earth smelled good to me, damp and rich. The colors of the flowers were dazzling.

Adam and I kept bumping elbows and shoulders. From time to time I glanced sideways, watching him search the flowers, studying the strong shape of his hands, the width of his wrists. Maybe he thought I was admiring his row of spring blooms—he picked a small bouquet of grape hyacinths and tucked them in the pocket of my jeans.

Neither of us said a word, but it was a different kind of silence than the cold wall that had once separated us. It was a quiet filled with sunlight. I started thinking I wouldn't mind crawling around like this all afternoon. Then Grizzly leaped to his feet, scrambling to the right of us.

"There it is!" he exclaimed. "I see it, Stacy!"

She rose quickly. "Are you sure?"

"I caught it sparkling out of the corner of my eye."

111

He reached down and triumphantly plucked up the diamond. It glittered like cold fire at the tip of his fingers.

"Phew!" I said, sitting back on my heels.

"I was starting to worry," Adam admitted.

Stacy stood before Coach and lifted her left hand. He slipped the ring on her finger, sliding it down slowly, his eyes on the ring. Then he glanced up and saw how she was looking at him.

"Everything's okay now," he said, his voice husky.

Stacy wrapped her arms around him. "Thank you . . . thank you."

Was it my imagination, or did they both hold on a little too long for a thank-you hug? Had I really seen Coach close his eyes for a second?

"Well," I murmured, standing up and brushing off my knees. Adam stood up beside me.

"I should get going," Grizzly said, suddenly letting go of Stacy. "See you two at school," he told Adam and me, then strode straight through a bed of tulips, knocking off flurries of petals, as if he couldn't get to his car fast enough.

Stacy watched him until he disappeared through the hedge gate. "I better go too," she said. "I'm supposed to drop off Travis's revised list of songs at the bandleader's house."

Adam and I walked her as far as the tall hedge.

"Thanks again, guys," she said. "Travis would never have forgiven me."

"No problem," Adam replied, pushing open the gate for her.

I followed Stacy, but Adam caught me by the belt loop and pulled me back inside the garden. He held the latch and closed the gate very softly. "That's how you do it when you don't want people to hear you," he said, smiling at me. "Can we talk a minute?"

"Sure."

He sat down on a small bench that was surrounded by lilacs. I stood awkwardly for a moment, realizing that the two of us were alone, then told myself to get real and sat down next to him.

"This is going to sound strange," Adam said, thrusting his feet out in front of him, studying them. "You'll probably think I'm crazy, but I was wondering if you noticed anything about—or between—Stacy and—"

"Coach?"

"You saw it too?" he asked, turning to me quickly.

"Even when they first met. But I don't know how to read the two of them."

Adam nodded and for a moment looked as if he was trying to read me.

"I'm not really sure how to interpret the way they look at each other," I went on.

He kept looking at me, and I pulled on my hair self-consciously, brushing out lilac blossoms that had drifted down, and babbled on nervously.

"The problem is, I don't have much experience with real—well—"

"What?" he asked.

"Love." The word came out so quietly, I thought

I'd have to say it again. But Adam's eyes flicked down to my mouth, so I guessed he'd read it off my lips.

"I know Stacy better than anyone," I told him. "But I don't know if she's really in love with Travis—"

Adam moved his face closer to mine, as if he couldn't hear me.

"—or if she's falling for Coach." I raised my voice. "I mean, what are the signs?"

"What are the signs for you?" he asked, his eyes shining with the soft green light I'd seen in them once before.

"Uh . . . I guess the same as for everybody else," I replied, dodging the question.

He sat back a little. "I think in some ways Stacy and Travis are good for each other," he said. "They balance each other. She's warm and friendly—spontaneous. He's serious, conservative, the money-earner type. When they got engaged, they fit my pet theory—I've always thought love was a lot of hype," Adam explained, "the spin people gave to a practical arrangement, nothing more." He leaned forward, dropping his hands loosely in front of him. "Now I'm not so sure."

I stared at his long back. Something—maybe the fragrance of the lilacs—was making me incredibly light-headed.

"I'm not sure either," I said. "There's something about the way Coach touches her."

Adam glanced over his shoulder at me. The long glance felt like a touch.

"What do you think we should do?" I asked.

"I don't know." He straightened up, which brought his face closer to mine again.

What was going on with me? I was like some kind of sonar device, always registering how close or far he was.

"You know," he said suddenly, "the lilacs make your gray eyes look violet."

I blinked at him with surprise, then we both looked away.

"I wish Stacy would postpone the wedding, just to make sure," I told him.

Adam nodded. "I wish that Coach would ask her to, but I think he's too much like me. When it comes to relationships, I've always been a low-risk guy. I never take on girls who are a challenge. Maybe I've missed out," he added, a lopsided smile lighting his face. "Or maybe I've spared myself a lot of trouble."

"Probably the latter."

"What do you do," he asked, "when you keep thinking about someone you never thought you'd glance at twice?"

I looked up slowly, meeting his eyes.

"I don't think Coach is the kind of guy Stacy had in mind," he said, "not for a husband. As for Coach, I don't think he was looking for anybody."

I nodded in agreement.

"But something has happened between them." Adam was silent for a moment. "What are you supposed to do," he asked, his voice growing deep

115

and soft, "when you find yourself unexpectedly falling for someone?"

"I—I really don't know," I replied, pulling my eyes from his and rising quickly from the bench. "But I sure hope they do."

TWELVE

IN THE NEXT two days I decided that Adam and I were wrong about the romantic feelings brewing between Coach and Stacy—at least, wrong about Stacy. When I talked to her Sunday night, she told me she planned to come to Tuesday's lacrosse game, which was at her old high school, and would bring cookies for Tilson's team as a thank-you to Coach and Adam. But she never showed.

That evening, when she stopped by our house, she asked about the game, explaining that she'd been so busy, it had slipped her mind. Then she showed Grandpa and me what she'd been busy with, spreading out on the dining-room table the floor plans of her and Travis's new house—a place big enough to raise a scout troop. She pulled out wallpaper samples and fabric swatches, as well as photos of all the expensive furniture they were purchasing. I doubted Coach could have afforded one piece. Stacy chattered on about her and Travis's plans, as she had for the last six months; things hadn't changed for her.

No, I was the one who was feeling and acting different. Late that night I received an E-mail from Daniel saying he'd changed his mind and wanted to come to the dance as well as the wedding. I wasn't mad, but I wasn't glad. Daniel was simply irrelevant.

Then Wednesday afternoon, working in the *Pipeline* office, I realized that I wasn't writing like myself. I'd assigned last Friday's lacrosse game to Vinny and yesterday's victory to myself. But the write-ups seemed reversed. Where had those zingers come from in Vinny's piece? Had he learned from me too well? My article was equally bewildering. The guys had played poorly in the first half of the game, and Adam had seemed distracted. But instead of criticizing them, I'd explained how our team got off on the wrong foot. Was I seeing and understanding more—or was I making excuses for them? Was I cutting Adam a well-deserved break—or was I losing my edge?

I stared hard at my computer screen.

"You okay, Jane?" Tom asked, breaking in on my thoughts.

"Huh?" I looked around. Everyone else had left. "Yeah, why?"

"Well, for one thing, you're not sitting in the right chair."

"No wonder I can't think," I said, jumping up to get my wheels.

I barely met deadline.

That evening when I got home, I wanted to talk to Grandpa, but I was too embarrassed. Despite the friendship between Marnie and me, I'd never had difficulty writing about the girls' team, so I didn't want to admit I was struggling to remain objective about the guys. Grandpa would never understand—I knew he'd never felt a strange happiness bubbling up in him when the Colts' middle linebacker brushed against him.

I have to get over this, I told myself. No one would guess I'd fallen for the guy I'd once taken shots at. Certainly not the target himself.

But what if Adam was seeing me differently too? I knew that all kinds of girls were interested in him. What kind of girl was he drawn to?

I couldn't believe I was wondering about these things instead of why the team had played a 2-1-1-2 offense when the 2-1-3 was more suited to our strengths.

Marnie came over that evening to work on a Spanish project with me. I was dying to talk about Adam but not quite ready to. I'd eventually confess how I felt to Marnie; chances were she'd already guessed.

We worked for a solid hour on our project, then took a break, sitting cross-legged on my bedroom floor, throwing M&M's in the air and catching them with our mouths.

"Did you talk to Kelly today?" Marnie asked between gulps.

"She was in the news office after school, running her mouth as usual. I've learned to tune her out."

"So you didn't hear her talking about the dance," Marnie said.

"Nope. Did I miss a big scoop?"

Marnie hesitated. "This isn't a scoop," she replied, "but when I saw Josh in chem lab today, I asked him to the dance."

"Cool!" I exclaimed. "He is *so* nice, Marn. You'd make a great couple."

"Don't get carried away. We're just friends."

I wiggled my finger in the bag, trying to get out the last few candies. "So? You never know where being friends can lead to. Is that what Kelly's spreading around?"

"No. She's spreading the news about her date with Adam."

It felt like a giant-sized candy had just gotten stuck in my throat. "Adam . . . and Kelly?" I swallowed hard.

Marnie nodded.

"Well," I said, "that's a surprise." *He can't like Kelly! He can't be a sucker for the compliments of a ditz!*

But obviously he did and he was. "Did she ask him or he ask her?"

"I don't know, but I'll find out," Marnie replied.

All jocks want is adoration, I thought. "No. No, don't bother," I said aloud. "Well, it looks like we're all going with dates. Daniel E-mailed me a second time and said he's coming after all."

Marnie looked surprised. "Do you want him to?"

"Sure. Can't wait."

"Jane," she said, catching my hand before I tossed and swallowed another candy, "you're just no good at lying."

"Where have you been?" Vinny demanded Friday afternoon when I arrived at the guys' lacrosse game five minutes after it had started.

"Back at the office," I told him. "Tom said you were out here, so I didn't worry."

"*I* worried," said Vinny. "It's good to have two sets of eyes, one pair to see what the other pair missed."

He was quoting me from our first few games together.

"But your eyes aren't missing much anymore," I replied. "You did a great job on your last article. Tom thought so too."

"Yeah?" He rubbed his hand over his short, bristly hair.

"Yeah! You didn't just describe, you analyzed. And you worked your quotes in well and—what was that—what happened?" I asked when the ref blew his whistle.

"Red in the crease," he replied. "Aren't you supposed to be keeping your eyes on the game?"

At the beginning of the season I'd reminded Vinny over and over that he could talk to me without looking at me—he was always to keep his eyes on the action. Now I climbed up on the bleacher behind him so I could watch the game *and* Kelly, who was sitting about ten feet to the left of us. What did Adam see in her? I mean, besides the huge eyes, the full, round mouth, and the enchanted look she could get on her face? I couldn't believe how jealous I was.

I forced myself to focus on the game. Our offense worked the ball around, then Adam sent a screaming pass into Pablo, who quick-sticked it into the net. I whooped with the crowd.

"Jane, you're beating on my back."

"Oh. Sorry."

"Adam should probably have taken that shot," Vinny said. "Pablo has scored twice, and they're keying in on him. Adam was in the clear. A strong shot from him, even if blocked, would have taken the pressure off Pablo, spread the defense more. Don't you think?"

"Vinny, did you memorize *everything* I told you?"

"I'm trying to learn," he said.

At halftime I told Vinny to interview whatever players he thought important. I got blurbs from the coaches.

I spent the second half trying to see the game from the bleachers where Vinny and I were sitting, but I kept seeing the action through Adam's eyes. It felt as if every defenseman that checked him checked me. I felt every bang and knock. Every shot he took, I took, willing the ball past the feet of the goalie. It was a relief when the game was over.

"We'll do follow-ups from halftime," I told

Vinny, and hightailed it to the coach of the opposing team. I got some good quotes, and for a moment I felt like myself again. Then, on my way back to Grizzly, I passed Adam and Kelly.

"Quarter to eight?" I heard Adam ask.

"Five of," she said, smiling. "We don't want to arrive too early."

I knew they were talking about the dance. Unfortunately Grizzly turned away at that moment to greet a parent. I quickly pretended to read my notes.

"Hi, Jane," Kelly said. "We were just talking about tonight."

"Good."

"Are you going to the dance?" she asked.

"Yes." I flipped a page in my notebook, though I hadn't read a word of it.

"We are too," she told me.

"Great."

"I guess you're waiting to interview Adam," she said to me, then laid her hand on his arm. "We can talk tonight," she told him.

I glanced up as far as the number on Adam's jersey. "Vinny's covering players. He'll be around soon."

"Why Vinny?" He leaned sideways to block me when I tried to move on, lowering his head until I looked at him.

"Because he wants to learn and is doing a good job."

"Not the same kind of job as you," Adam replied. "You know you're the best."

I pulled curly shreds of paper from the spiral of my notebook. Wonderful. I'd finally gotten his respect for me as a reporter just when I wanted something else.

"Thanks. I see Vinny heading this way. Hey, Coach!" I called, chasing after him before another parent got hold of him. I spent a lot of time questioning Grizzly that day. What I really wanted to ask was, "Are you as miserable as I am?" but we stuck to lacrosse.

Josh walked me back to the school building. I wondered if Marnie had said something to him because he draped his arm casually around my shoulders and told jokes on the way, as if he was trying to cheer me up.

Pablo passed by and gave me a high five. Jordy did the same. Yeah, the team accepted me now, respected me now. Heck, I was like one of the guys.

It was enough to make a tough girl cry.

THIRTEEN

D ANIEL ARRIVED AN hour late that evening, which was no surprise to me.

"Looking good, Jane," Daniel said when I opened the door.

I hoped so. I was beginning to have second thoughts about the outfit Marnie had talked me into, a very short skirt with opaque stockings and a skimpy kind of top. I'd added a pair of earrings that Angela had given me, big-dangle jobs like the kind I was always admiring on her.

"Come in a sec and say hello," I invited. "Hey, Mom? Grandpa?"

Grandpa rose from the couch to shake Daniel's hand, studying him with the interested eyes of a reporter.

Daniel's hair was several inches longer than mine and pulled back in a ponytail with thin braids woven through it. He wore full-cut pants and a

125

long, oversize shirt that was collarless and open at the top, accentuating the multicolored necklace he wore. Fortunately for Daniel he was a big guy with a good-looking face, so he could get away with things like funky jewelry.

Mom came in from the kitchen to greet Daniel and told him how much she liked the beads around his neck. We left before she got a good view of the new tattoo on his left ear.

Daniel had driven his old family station wagon, which looked as if it had traveled cross-country several times—pulled by oxen. Tonight the backseat of the wagon was filled with shirts, pants, and underwear.

"What are the clothes for?" I asked.

"To wear," Daniel replied. "I didn't have time to pack a suitcase, so I just threw them in the car. Actually, I didn't have time to do laundry either," he added as he pulled out of the parking space. "But Aunt Katie's a sweetheart—she won't mind washing them."

"You're staying at her house this weekend?"

He nodded. "Aunt Margaret won't have me back. You know, I'm glad we're doing this," Daniel said. "I've missed hanging out with you."

"Really?"

"My parents are glad," he explained. "They think you're a good influence on me."

"Oh."

"They wish I'd date more ordinary girls," he went on.

"Ordinary?"

"They like you because, well, they think you've got your head on straight."

"I see. Turn right at the stop sign."

He did, without stopping first, without looking to see if a car was coming from the left. The unhappy driver of that car, who had the right-of-way, blasted us with his horn.

"What I'm saying," he went on, "is that at the School of Arts we're all, like, flying into passions. You never know who's going to do what. But you, Jane—you're nice and reliable."

I winced.

"You're the kind of girl a guy can count on."

"You mean because I stop at stop signs?"

"Some of the girls at school, they're fantastic," he continued.

I wished he'd keep his eyes on the road.

"Totally fantastic, morphing all the time, but they wear me out. Not you. At camp last summer I always knew where you were coming from. In your E-mails too. You're always Jane."

Daisy, I felt like telling him. "Turn left." I sighed.

"That's why I decided to come tonight. I kept thinking about how it was at camp, not wild or anything, just kind of easy and sweet. You're good for me."

"We're here," I said bleakly.

I'd hoped that having a date and dressing differently would give me confidence when I met up with Kelly and Adam. Now I felt as attractive and exciting as a nun.

Daniel and I parked and slipped into the gym during a slow dance. It was dark, so it was hard to see who was with whom. Some couples swayed with their heads on each other's shoulders; others were shyer and danced a little straighter and stiffer. I noticed a couple who'd been turning clockwise suddenly turn in the opposite direction, as if the guy wanted a second look at Daniel and me. The guy was Adam.

A moment later Kelly twisted her head around to see who Adam was looking at, then gave me a little wave. I waved back and turned quickly to Daniel. "Let's dance."

As soon as Daniel and I found the rhythm, I closed my eyes. I wasn't feeling romantic; I just didn't want to see Kelly and Adam. I guess I should've realized that Daniel would lead pretty much the way he drove. We hadn't been swaying long when we plowed into another couple, Pablo and his girl.

"Sorry, Pablo," I said.

He glanced from me to Daniel, looking Daniel up and down as if my date had just landed from another universe.

The song faded and the lights came on, making everyone blink for a moment. The band was taking a break, and people started heading out of the gym. I spotted Marnie and Josh across the way and pulled Daniel in their direction, dragging him away from Kelly and Adam and several other guys on the lacrosse team who were staring at him. Marnie and Josh met us halfway.

"Hi, Daniel!" she greeted him. She looked great in her tight pants and midriff top. "We've been looking for you two."

"Just got here," I told her, then introduced the guys to each other.

Josh studied Daniel's ear for a moment. "Is that a tattoo or stitches?"

Daniel wasn't offended. "A tattoo that's supposed to look like stitches."

"Oh."

"It symbolizes creation," Daniel explained, "the cutting and healing of it, the stitching together of old and damaged things in a new way."

Josh looked at Daniel as if he were crazy.

"Sooo, how about getting some air?" I suggested, and we made our way to the wide set of steps outside the building.

I knew that with Josh there, some of the guys from the lacrosse team might come over to talk, but I never expected the reaction we got. They checked out Daniel from head to foot. I suddenly had a half dozen "big brothers" who wanted to know who I was dating and what he was like. In a matter of minutes we'd formed a large group on the school steps. Daniel ate up the attention, talking about life in Washington, his school, and the cool stuff he and his friends did.

I remembered how exciting his life had seemed the first time I heard about it at camp. But I'd heard the same thing several times over now, and it was getting boring. I wanted to escape but was stuck in the middle of the crowd, so I sat down, enjoying a bit of solitude in the forest of legs.

A minute later Adam's face peered at me between some of those legs. He'd also sat down on the steps. "How's it going, Jane?"

"Okay. How about for you?"

"Okay."

"Good game today," I told him. "The whole team is playing solid ball."

He moved his head to one side as Kelly reached down to scratch her leg. "I didn't see you there at the beginning," he said.

"Oh, well, I had stuff to do in the office." I shifted around. Daniel was leaning against me, his hand resting on the top of my head.

Adam glanced upward at him, then said, "So how's Stacy doing?"

"She's all excited about the new house and the furniture she and Travis have picked out. I think maybe we were wrong about her and Coach."

"Maybe."

We sat in silence for a few moments.

"Those are different clothes than you usually wear," Adam observed.

I pulled my legs up a step and wrapped my arms around them, feeling self-conscious.

"Sort of artsy looking, I guess," he added. "Artsy and different."

"I don't have to dress the same way every day."

"No," he replied, "but I like the way you usually dress."

"I don't dress according to what guys like," I said quickly.

He shrugged. "I was just curious about why you changed."

"Does it bother you? Do you like to think of me as reliable? A girl you can always count on to be the same? Good old ordinary Jane?"

He looked bewildered. "What do you mean?"

"Oh, never mind," I said, standing up suddenly and almost knocking Daniel off his step.

"Girl, you look hot," Angela said to me.

She and Tom had joined our group. He was talking to Daniel.

"Thanks, Angela. I needed to hear that."

Out of the corner of my eye I saw Adam's head pop up between people as he rose to his feet.

"Those dangles look fabulous," she added.

"Yeah, the person who picked them out has great taste." I leaned closer to her. "Where's you-know-who?" I whispered, referring to Tom's college girlfriend.

"Had a big paper due. What a shame," Angela said softly, then smiled an incredible smile.

The band began playing again, and everyone started to drift back toward the gym. Daniel and I climbed the steps with the others, then I felt Kelly at my elbow. She put her arm around my waist as if we were best buddies. "He is so cool," she said to me.

I looked at her blankly for a moment.

"He's so different," she explained, "so intriguing."

"Oh, you mean Daniel."

She laughed as if I'd been playing dumb. "You make a really great couple."

Daniel turned to her and smiled. Adam, who was trailing her and listening in, wore no expression at all.

I was glad to get inside the dark gym. I danced every song with Daniel, hoping to lose myself in the music, hoping to forget that Adam was dancing with someone else. The gym grew more crowded as kids who came stag stopped by. The chaperons were kept busy with couples making out in the corners. We were wall-to-wall and steamy when the band announced its second break.

I checked my watch. *One more hour,* I thought, hoping it would pass quickly, then someone tapped me on the shoulder. "Mind if I have this dance?" Marnie asked.

Daniel looked flattered.

"No problem," I said. I stepped back to see if Josh was free, but he'd already taken Kelly by the arm.

That left Adam. The two of us stood there looking around as if we'd never been to a dance before and didn't know what to do with ourselves. Then he smiled and walked over.

"Looks like you're stuck with me," he said.

The music started, one of those tear-jerking movie theme songs, and we began dancing awkwardly. He held me as if I were made of glass and left enough space for a third person to dance between us.

"This is really uncomfortable," I said after a minute of the worst dancing I'd ever experienced. I could see Marnie laughing at us.

"I'm not sure how to do it with you," Adam confessed.

"The same as you'd do it with any girl."

"I'll probably step on your foot," he said. "And I've already banged you up once."

"With a lacrosse stick," I reminded him. "You're not hiding one somewhere, are you?"

"No." He pulled me closer, then closer again, glancing at me twice as if to make sure it was okay.

My body was almost touching his. I could feel his arms around my back, one hand resting lightly against it. Who'd have thought that such a barely touching, shuffling-back-and-forth dance could make me all quivery inside? We kept this up for another minute.

Suddenly I saw Josh and Kelly veering into us. I pulled back a little, but at that same moment we got slammed from the other side by Marnie and Daniel, sandwiched between the two couples. Adam instinctively held me tight, his one hand cupping my head protectively.

"Oh, sorry," Marnie said, sounding in no way sincere.

Both couples moved away, but Adam's hand still held my head against his chest. I could feel his long fingers in my hair. I got goose bumps all over. *Don't let go,* I thought, *don't let go.*

He didn't. We danced and he held me tight, his arms wrapped warm and strong around me. I felt him lower his chin, moving his face closer to mine. I don't know when I shut my eyes. When I opened them, he was looking at me intently, his face so near to mine, I could see the curl of every golden eyelash.

His eyes cast some kind of spell on me. He was looking at my mouth. That ache I felt on April nights was finally becoming defined. It had a focus: Adam's mouth, Adam's kiss.

"Daisy," he said softly.

Then the music stopped. It was as if the magic carpet beneath me had been suddenly jerked away and I plummeted to earth.

The lights came on and I pulled away, feeling shaky all over. I was in deep, way too deep. Where was Daniel?

"Daniel?" I said, turning around quickly. "Daniel?" I wanted to leave.

As soon as I snatched him from a startled Marnie, I suggested to him that we take off. "Let's go somewhere else," I said, "somewhere where all these people aren't."

"Hang loose, Jane," he told me. "There'll be time to fool around later."

Adam, who'd been reclaimed by Kelly, looked over at me with cold green eyes. What was his problem? I wasn't his date—just how many girls did he want to kiss in one night?

We headed outside again, where I had the pleasure of watching him and Kelly slip from the view of a chaperon and head across the playing fields in the direction of the bridge.

An hour later I got to watch them slow dance to the most romantic song of the evening. They looked perfectly in sync, with Adam's eyes closed the entire time. As if that weren't bad enough, my miserable view of them was continually interrupted by Daniel, who was trying like mad to make out with me. Where was a chaperon when you needed one? The old nose block lost its effectiveness on the third attempt. His lips met mine and stuck there. The kiss was as uninspiring as the good-night embraces I remembered from camp. I came down hard on his foot. "Oops," I said sweetly.

The short ride home lasted forever. We talked about Daniel, and Daniel, and Daniel—his artwork and his dreams for the future. We spent a half hour parked in front of my house, talking about the same—which, of course, was preferable to kissing him. But when he saw me fumbling with the door handle, he swung into action.

"Sorry," he apologized, reaching for my face, turning it back toward him. "You get me so wound up, talking about stuff. You're such a great listener and all, you make me forget what girls are always waiting for."

"I'm not waiting for anything, Daniel."

He pulled me closer. It was as if he couldn't hear anything *he* didn't say.

"Daniel, listen to me—I'm taking back the invitation to the wedding."

"The wedding will be a bore," he agreed, "but we can cut out early and have some fun."

"No, no, we can't." I pushed him back a little. "Daniel, we're not really a match."

"I know. We're opposites, but you're so good for me."

"Maybe . . . but you know what? You're not good for *me*. And that counts too."

He looked at me with a confused, almost child-like expression.

I patted his hand. "Good night."

FOURTEEN

A T ELEVEN-THIRTY on Saturday morning, three hours past my natural waking time, I finally made it downstairs. Grandpa was sitting at the kitchen bar, reading recipes and making a grocery list. I opened a cupboard, pulled out a box of croutons, stared at it uncomprehendingly, then put it back and took out my cereal.

"Should I ask how the dance went?" Grandpa inquired.

"I wouldn't if I were you."

"Want to hear the morning headlines?"

"Sure."

"Your mom's gone off to the mall, Marnie has called twice, Stacy is over at Coach's—dropping off cookies to thank him for last weekend's heroics—and the Orioles are going for their seventh in a row this afternoon." He smiled, then took his cookbook out on the back porch to read. Grandpa knew when to leave me alone and how to find a place to hang out in case I suddenly wanted company.

I poured my cereal and started spooning it down dry, then dumped some sugar on the already sweetened flakes. The last time I'd glanced at my alarm clock the night before it had read 4:05 A.M., which meant I'd spent at least four hours thinking about Adam, reliving the dance with him, remembering how it was to look into his eyes and how it felt to have him gazing so intently into mine.

That look had to mean something, didn't it? It had to mean as much as a walk to the bridge with Kelly!

But then I'd remembered Billy's words when Adam was being interviewed by Kelly after our one-on-one match: "I've seen that look a million times. It's how Adam handles girls." During the last dance Adam had put his arms around Kelly and closed his eyes. Maybe when he *didn't* look, it meant something—it meant it was the real thing rather than a moment of flirting.

I'll get over this, I said to myself, sorting through the newspaper, looking for the sports section. Mixed in with sports was a single sheet of legal paper folded in half. I opened it up to a diagram, rotating the paper in my hands, trying to figure out what it was.

"Grandpa—" I carried my cereal and the diagram outside and sat down next to him on the top porch step. "What's this?"

"Let's see—oh, that's the seating chart for the wedding reception." He pointed to a long, rectangular block. "There's the head table, where you will be."

I read the names hand-printed on the chart. Adam and I were seated on either side of the bride and groom.

"Your mother and I will be making faces at you from over here," Grandpa added, pointing to a round table.

I saw that Daniel's name was written next to Mom and Grandpa's—I'd have to let Stacy know that had changed. My aunt and uncle were seated on the other side of Daniel. Next to Uncle Jake was another familiar name: Kelly! Adam had asked her to the wedding! I drew my breath in slowly and let it out again, trying to ease the tightness in my chest. Was I going to hurt like this every time I knew they were together?

"You're not looking forward to this, are you?" Grandpa asked.

"No. Are you?"

He shook his head.

"What's worrying you?" I asked.

"A lot of things," he replied. "You're on the list."

"What's worrying you about the wedding?" I said, not wanting to talk about me. "Do you have doubts about Stacy and Travis?"

He didn't answer right away. "Yes," he finally admitted, "but I learned long ago not to give unwanted advice and opinions to adult children. Now I'm learning all over again why it's so hard to keep your mouth shut. I hope Stacy is right and I'm wrong."

"That makes two of us," I said.

A few minutes later Marnie drove the family Jeep down the back alley, demonstrating the expertise of a resident who knew the potholes by heart. She parked behind Stacy's car, then hopped out.

"Sleeping Beauty!" she called.

"Try Sleeping Beastly," I answered back.

"Hey, Mr. O."

"Hi, Marnie," Grandpa said, then rose. "I'd better put this chart inside."

"I can't stay long—I have to pick up my brother from Little League," Marnie said when she sat down next to me. "Did you have a good time last night?"

"No," I replied honestly. "How about you?"

"Even better than I thought. Josh is a nice guy."

"Yeah? Any sparks?" I asked.

"Not yet. Maybe never. But a lot of laughs."

"By the way, that was a nice squeeze play you guys pulled off," I said.

Marnie wiggled one foot, then grinned at me. "We planned the dance-partner switch, but the squeeze play—that was more like reading a teammate's eyes from across the field and going for it."

I didn't respond.

"You two almost went for it," Marnie prompted.

I quivered inside just thinking about the almost kiss.

"What I don't get," she added, "is why you *did* go for it with Daniel. I thought you'd decided you'd had enough of him."

I looked up. "I did."

"You chose a funny way to send your message—

making out with him during the last dance."

"Obviously you missed the nose blocks."

"Actually, I missed it all," Marnie admitted. "Josh and I were on the other side of the gym. I got the scoop from the guys on the lacrosse team."

"What?"

"They said you and Daniel were making out through the entire last dance."

"No wonder they miss shots! They need their eyes checked!"

"Well, what's your story?" she asked.

"It's not a story; it's true. Daniel was on the move during the last dance, but I played defense. He scored once, very briefly, just before I stepped on his foot."

Marnie laughed. "Well," she said with a shrug, "I guess it's hard to see exactly what's going on in the dark. They saw a little and their imaginations filled in the rest."

"You don't tell everyone something happened when you're not sure what you saw!" I said angrily.

"The guys on the team care about you, Jane, that's all. Josh and I went out with some of them for pizza afterward, and they kept asking me about Daniel. They couldn't figure him out—couldn't figure you and him out."

"Was Adam there?"

"For a little while. He and Kelly left early."

"He and Kelly will be at the wedding next weekend," I told Marnie. "As for who was really making out, I doubt that the two of them were just out for a walk when I saw them heading toward the bridge."

"Why don't you ask him? Ask him if he likes her."

I stared at her. "Are you crazy?"

"You've never had trouble asking him questions before," she pointed out.

I didn't need her to remind me that I was changing. "I can't believe it—a group of jocks acting like little old gossips," I muttered.

At that moment Stacy walked out the door of Mrs. Bean's house.

"Hi, Marnie," Stacy said as she crossed the alley. "Got a message from Grizzly for you, Dais. He said if you and Vinny want to ride on the team bus Tuesday, there's room."

A month ago I would've loved it. Now the last thing I wanted to do was ride to and from the game with a bunch of guys who were starting to treat me like their kid sister.

"That's nice of him, but I can borrow Grandpa's car."

"No, you can't," came a voice from inside.

I turned around. "Sorry, Jane," Grandpa said through the screen door. "The car's going in for work on Tuesday. And I can't put it off because I have two appointments Wednesday."

"The game's after school, isn't it?" Stacy interjected. "I'll take you, Daisy."

I looked at her, surprised. "Don't you have a few things to do? I mean, you're getting married this week."

"Oh, Travis has everything organized," my cousin replied. "I'd really like to go to the game. Grizzly says it's going to be an exciting one. The other team is big and plays a very physical game. It could get rough."

Marnie looked at Stacy with surprise. "I didn't know you were interested in sports."

"Did Grizzly like the cookies?" Grandpa asked, coming out on the porch.

Stacy smiled, her cheeks dimpling and growing pink. "He ate seven of them while I was there. So what time do you want to be picked up?" she asked me.

We made arrangements, then she started back down the walk.

"Stacy," Grandpa called after her. "Your seating chart."

"Huh?"

He waved the paper at her, but she looked at him blankly.

"For your wedding, hon," he said.

"Oh. Oh, yeah."

Oh, help, I thought.

I saw Adam during school hours only once Monday. He looked as busy as I pretended to be, so all I had to say was hi. Josh caught me before history class on Tuesday and asked why I wasn't going on the team bus.

"Just easier not to," I told him.

That afternoon Stacy showed up in the school lot with cans of cookies. Vinny, a freshman photographer named Mike, and I climbed into her car and talked sports most of the way to the game. Stacy listened as she drove, unusually quiet.

I had two things working in my favor in terms of covering that game. Since we were far from school, I wasn't distracted by the presence of Kelly and other adoring fans from Tilson. And it was Mike's first time shooting lacrosse, so working with him kept me plenty occupied.

The game itself was a rough one, just as Coach had predicted. The other team's defense was extremely aggressive, and we got rattled at first. I got rattled whenever they went after Adam. Tilson fought back hard and we went ahead in the third quarter, then lost by one heartbreaking goal. Afterward I had the awful, unprofessional desire to run onto the field and hug Adam. As the team collected its equipment, I saw Stacy put her hand lightly on Grizzly's shoulder, then Adam's, and wished I could do the same.

"Tough game," was all I said to him. Adam looked tired and beaten. He barely glanced at me. I felt miserable for him, but what could I do? I assigned Vinny the interview.

Wednesday, during our last period before early dismissal, I sat down to write an article on the defeat. Vinny and I had agreed that he'd write up Friday's game and I'd do yesterday's. I had a lot of notes to work from and began the article typing a million miles an hour, but when I stopped to read my first few paragraphs, I came to a screeching halt. Was I really starting to sound like Kelly? I clicked the mouse and punched keys—insert, delete, insert, delete—then read through the paragraphs again. If readers didn't know the final score, they'd think Tilson had won. Cripe—they'd think Adam had played the best game of his career!

I put aside the piece and worked on the rest of the sports page. Vinny's writing was really coming along, I noted with satisfaction, and Ellen was doing some first-rate stuff on our tennis teams. Sam was steady with the baseball coverage. I was the one floundering. I took another look at my article, then set it down again, disgusted.

By noontime I had the sports page put together except for my piece. The dismissal bell rang, and the halls swelled with kids. Angela and Tom came into the office with other staff members. I could hear Kelly chattering in the hall.

I spun around in my chair. "I have to get out of here," I said to Tom.

He looked at me, surprised.

"My page is done except for my own piece, and I'm getting nowhere on it here. Can I E-mail it from home?"

"Want to talk about it first?" he asked. "Want me to take a look at it?"

Kelly had come in and was digging through her mailbox.

"No." It came out a little too sharply.

"Okay, send it over by five forty-five," he said. "Phone before then if you need help."

"Thanks." I threw everything in my backpack and headed out the door.

"Jane, wait," Kelly called after me. "I've been looking for you. I haven't seen you since Friday night."

Apparently she hadn't noticed me ducking behind Marnie and stepping into classroom doorways when I spotted her coming down the hall.

"Did you have a good time with that gorgeous guy you were with?" Kelly asked. "Are you and he serious?"

"A good time?" I echoed. "I guess you could say it was a dance I won't soon forget." The feeling of Adam's mouth so close to mine was still haunting me.

"That's exactly the way I feel," Kelly said. "A night to remember always."

"A nightmare is more like it," I mumbled under my breath as I bolted out of the office.

On the way home I figured out a way to get my column written. First I'd write a "Kelly" article: I'd say all the positive, admiring, gushy things about Adam and his teammates that were bubbling up inside me. Then I'd write a second article, an analysis of the game from a negative point of view. I'd treat the second piece like a writing exercise—do it like the essay our English class had to write when we were studying satire—even force myself to take some unfair shots. Once I had the two contrasting views on paper, I'd weave together the most reasonable statements from each and produce a balanced column.

It would be a lot of work, but I'd do it. I'd get this piece written if I had to cut it out and paste it together word by word, letter by letter. No guy, no crazy romantic dreams, would keep me from doing my job!

FIFTEEN

THERE! THE SECOND article was done. Save and exit. Now I had two versions of yesterday's game, written by Dr. Jekyll and Mr. Hyde. I glanced at my watch: just three o'clock. Before trying to blend the two different perspectives into a fair analysis, I'd give myself a well-deserved break.

I headed outside to shoot baskets. Grandpa was at his doctor's appointment, Mom at work, and the little kids of our neighborhood still in school. It was peaceful in the back alley, with nothing but the sounds of birds twittering and the ball thumping on the concrete, its friendly bang and swish through the basket.

I missed a shot and the ball bounced into Mrs. Bean's yard, rolling under her forsythia. I followed it into the yard, then got down on my knees to retrieve it from under the bush.

"Big Mama!"

From far back in the branches the cat stared at me

with large, unfocused eyes. She was lying on her side, her front paw was oozing blood, and there was more blood on her hindquarters. Her tail was a dark, wet mess. She looked as if she'd been attacked by another animal, chased and bitten several times. When she tried to lift her head, it wobbled. She gazed at me helplessly, then dropped her chin in the dirt again.

Panicked, I ran to Mrs. Bean's door and pounded on it, hoping she was home, hoping she could help me get Mama to a vet. I rang her bell, then screamed up at the window. No response. Coach was at practice and the school office shut down. Marnie would also be out on the playing field. I ran home and called Stacy. I couldn't have been coherent, but somehow she figured out what I was saying.

I was back at the bush, talking gently to Big Mama, when the Saturn came flying down the alley. Stacy had thought to bring a soft quilt, a shower present still lying in its silver gift box. We worked the quilt under Big Mama as gently as we could, then lifted her up and laid her in the box.

"Has she lost a lot of blood?" Stacy asked.

"I don't know. How much blood do cats have in them? She's breathing really fast."

"She might be in shock," Stacy said. We wrapped the blanket gently around the cat to keep her warm.

I rode in the backseat with the box next to me, trying to hold it steady. Stacy ran a red light and nearly did a two-wheeler into the parking lot but got us to the vet in one piece.

We carried her in the entrance of the building as

fast as we could without jarring the box. I guess the look on our faces told the guy at the desk all he needed to know. He took us straight back to an examining room. "I'll get Dr. Grefe," he said.

When we lowered the box onto the examining table, Big Mama meowed pitifully. Stacy ran a finger behind the cat's ear, trying to soothe her.

"Where's Grizzly?" she asked me.

"At practice. At school."

"I'd better get him. You stay here."

As Stacy was on her way out, Dr. Grefe came in. He was a big man with a beard and warm blue eyes. "Let's see what we've got here," he said, his voice calm. "What's your cat's name?"

"Big Mama," I croaked.

"Big Mama," he crooned. "Looks like you got into some nasty stuff, Big Mama." He examined her as he talked. He glanced up at me. "Do you know what happened today?"

I shook my head. "She's my neighbor's cat. He was out. I found her under a bush."

Dr. Grefe examined the bloody tail. "I'd say Big Mama took on a dog."

An assistant came in then, and he gave the young woman instructions. To me he said, "How about waiting outside while we clean her up and take a closer look? I'll call you if we need you—promise."

I nodded and walked back to the waiting room. I didn't realize how badly my hands were shaking until I tried to pick up a magazine.

About fifteen minutes later Coach and Stacy

arrived, his face looking pale beneath his outdoor ruddiness. The desk clerk took him back to see the vet.

"Grizzly's a mess," Stacy told me. "If anything happens to Big Mama, he's going to need some gluing together."

"She's not my cat and *I'm* going to need gluing together," I replied.

We sat silently side by side in the plastic chairs, shifting uncomfortably as we waited. The bells on the door jingled each time an owner came in or out with a pet. It was a busy place with several vets, and after a while I stopped bothering to look up. Then someone sat down on the other side of me. His hand hovered over my balled-up fists, then touched me lightly on the knuckles. "How's Mama?" Adam asked.

"We don't know yet," I said. "The vet thinks she tangled with a dog."

"Grizzly's back there," Stacy added.

Adam ran one finger gently over the back of my hand. "It must have been scary to find her. How are you doing?"

"Okay."

Coach came out then, and all three of us looked up for the news.

"They're stitching her back together," he said. "She may lose her tail—it's a wait-see on that. They're hoping there are no internal injuries or complications, but they can't be sure yet." His voice sounded upbeat, but when he sat down next to Stacy, his body sagged.

150

Stacy shyly placed her hand on top of Coach's. He turned his over, palm up, and their fingers intertwined. I peeked at their hands, looking at how her slim hand was wrapped in his, how they gave each other comfort.

Adam caught me looking, and for a moment our eyes met and held. Looking in his eyes, I wondered if I was ever going to get over him. Then I sat back and folded my arms in front of me. Every time the door opened between the examining-room area and waiting room, the four of us looked up, hoping to get good news. But the wait dragged on. At about quarter to five the bells of the outside door jingled and Travis entered. I guess we were all staring at the worn tile floor because none of us noticed him at first.

"Travis!" Stacy said when he stood before her.

I glanced quickly to the left and saw her and Coach let go of each other's hands.

"How'd you know where I was?"

"I didn't at first," he replied, his voice low and controlled. "I started wondering when the bridal salon called my office. Twice. You were supposed to pick up your veil and headpiece. Then the caterer called, wanting to know the final guest count—apparently you forgot to inform him. Then my stepmother called and said Adam had followed you to a vet's on York Road, so he wouldn't be picking up the ushers' gifts till later tonight. This is the third vet I've been to on York Road."

"Why?" Stacy asked.

"Why?" He was close to exploding. "We have a

few things to do. We're getting married Saturday, or did that slip your mind?"

Several people in the waiting room, including the desk attendant, cocked their heads, listening with interest.

"Tomorrow night's the bachelor party," he continued. "The next night, the rehearsal. When do you think we're going to get these things done?"

"It was an emergency," Stacy explained. "Grizzly's cat was attacked by a dog. Once we know that Big Mama's okay, I'll get to things."

"It's not an emergency, Stacy, it's a cat. And it's not even your cat!"

Her eyes sparked. "How could it be?" she replied. "You said I couldn't have one."

All the people with cat carriers turned to looked reproachfully at Travis.

"You said they're unfriendly and sneaky."

The stares got ugly.

"And we can't have a dog," she continued, "because they smell bad."

The dog owners began to scowl at him.

I leaned toward Adam. "Travis had better get out of this place while there's still time."

"Come on, Travis," Adam said, standing up. "You pick up the cuff links. I'll get the headgear. Where's the salon, Stacy?"

She told him, then Adam pushed his stepbrother out the door, followed by dirty looks from everyone in the waiting room.

I glanced at the clock. Five-fifteen. I couldn't

leave without knowing whether Mama was going to be okay, but I had to get in my article by quarter to six.

Ten minutes later Dr. Grefe's assistant came to the door and called us in. I hoped for Grizzly's sake that they hadn't found something serious.

The vet smiled at us as we entered the room. "She's a tough old girl," he said.

Mama was looking patchy, her tail hairless and thin as a rat's, her fur shaved cleanly from a spot on her back end as well as one leg, where they'd sewn her up.

"As I told you before, she sustained a nasty bite on the tail, and we're going to have to see how that goes. I want to keep her here for twenty-four hours of observation, but I think an animal heals best in its home. Check in with me tomorrow. If she's doing all right, you can pick her up at five. I'll show you how to do her dressing and bandaging, and we'll make a follow-up appointment."

"Can I come a little later than that?" Grizzly asked. "I coach a team, then take a class on Thursday evening till seven-thirty."

"Sorry. We close at seven."

"I'll pick her up, Grizzly," Stacy offered, "and stay with her till you get home. I can find out what to do and teach you."

"But don't you have to—whatever it is brides do?"

"I'll be here at five," Stacy told the vet. "Count on it."

Stacy insisted on driving me home. But what

she really wanted was to make sure Coach was okay. She dropped me off in the back alley, then parked and met Grizzly in Mrs. Bean's yard. I left the two of them to talk and raced inside to the computer.

With just five minutes till deadline there was no time to blend the contrasting views of the two articles and write a balanced column. And there was no way I'd send the satirical version with its harsh, somewhat unfair criticism of the team. That left me with the positive draft, the one that read as if Kelly had written it. I pulled up my document, typed in the E-mail address, and clicked on send. *Whew!*

As I pushed back my chair, I wondered who on the team would notice the new voice of Jane Hardy. Too bad I didn't notice which file I'd sent.

Sixteen

"**M**Y POWER SANDWICH!" Marnie exclaimed on Thursday at lunchtime. She felt inside her lunch bag again, then pulled out a jelly sandwich with its crusts cut off and a cellophane bag of happy-face cookies—her little brother's meal. "How am I going to play today without my power sandwich?" She looked over at my lunch. "Do you have anything better?"

"Help yourself. I don't want it."

"You're not on a diet, are you?" she teased, picking up my tuna on whole wheat.

"No."

"Pining away from unrequited love?"

"Marnie!"

She took a bite and chewed thoughtfully. "I think you should tell Adam how you feel."

"Keep your voice down, okay?" I glanced two tables over, where Kelly was sitting with a group of people.

"If you told him, what's the worst-possible thing that could happen?" Marnie asked.

"You mean other than my complete humiliation when he looks amazed, then laughs hysterically?"

"Adam's too nice a guy to do that," she replied.

"Okay, so he looks amazed, chokes back his laughter, and then feels sorry for me. That's worse."

"What an optimist you are!" she said. "Here, have a jelly sandwich and some cookies. Comfort food."

I took the bag, then looked around and saw that the latest edition of *The Pipeline* had already been stacked by the cafeteria entrances. Angela was handing out papers to Kelly and her friends. She came over to our table to drop off two copies. "Special delivery."

"Thanks, Ang."

"No problem," she replied, and moved on.

"Kelly's got headlines this week," Marnie said, spreading her copy on the table. "Front-page coverage of the dance."

I started working on Teddy's happy-face cookies.

"Hey, Jane, you're quoted here."

"Where?" I asked, popping another cookie in my mouth. They were stale, but chocolate was chocolate.

"In Kelly's column."

"I can't be," I said. "I've hardly spoken to her since Friday."

"Well, when you were speaking, did you happen to say, 'It was a dance I won't soon forget'?"

"Oh, yeah, I did say that when she asked me if I'd had a good time."

I picked up my copy of the paper and scanned the gossip column, which reported who went with whom and how everyone dressed in long, boring detail. Then I found it: "Jane Hardy came with a fantastic-looking artist from a school in Washington, D.C. When asked if she and he were something serious, she said simply, 'It was a dance I won't soon forget.'"

"Cripe!" I exclaimed. "Talk about splicing sentences together and giving things a different meaning! It sounds as if Daniel and I are in love. How could she do this to me?"

I tossed the cookies in the bag with the sandwich and crumpled them together, squeezing the bag hard.

"I doubt it's intentional," Marnie replied. "She just doesn't know what she's doing." She tapped me on the wrist. "Ease up, or we're going to have jelly squirting all over the place."

I shook my head in disbelief.

"Come on," Marnie said, shoving the rest of my tuna sandwich in her mouth. "I need to stop at my locker."

We gathered our stuff, dumped our trash, and headed out of the cafeteria. As we pushed through the doors, Josh and Adam were coming in.

"Hi," I said.

"Hi," Josh replied.

Adam stopped squarely in front of me. "I just read your column."

"Yeah?" I tried to sound casual, as if the piece I'd sweated blood over was no big deal.

"I thought it stunk."

I looked at him, stunned. "Excuse me?"

"It was unfair and dead wrong."

I blinked. I was too surprised to do anything else.

Marnie opened her copy of the paper to see what I'd written. When she bit her lip and glanced sideways at me rather than leaping to my defense, I began to read over her shoulder.

My heart sank. "It's the wrong draft. I E-mailed the wrong draft!"

"I told you there was an explanation," Josh said to Adam.

But Adam was really angry. "The wrong draft? Not quite the spin you wanted?" he asked. "Why can't writers just tell the truth?" His eyes blazed. "Is that too boring for you, Jane? Do you have to be the center of attention with your articles? You're always manipulating things, always trying to get a reaction!"

"I had another version," I began, "one that was really positive; I mean it was actually too—"

I broke off. How could I explain the situation without admitting my feelings for him?

"Too positive?" he finished the sentence for me. "I have trouble imagining that." There was more than anger in his eyes, a darker shade of something, but I didn't know what it was or what to say back. I saw him swallow hard.

In a quieter voice he said, "I don't understand you. I can't figure out what goes on inside your head." Then he walked away.

When the cafeteria door closed behind him and Josh, Marnie observed, "He'd be shocked to find out what's going on inside your heart."

I leaned back against the wall. "I can't believe I did that."

I told her why I'd written the different drafts, but she knew me so well, she'd already guessed.

Later that afternoon I came clean with Tom. Talk about embarrassing! His handpicked sports editor falling for a jock and unable to keep her head on straight! I told him what I thought we should do, and he said it was my decision. He also did his best to shore up my self-respect, which was abysmal at that point. An hour later, while Vinny and I were covering the girls' game, I told him that he was now full-time reporter for guys' lacrosse. The column was his baby.

"You mean—every game?" Vinny asked, surprised.

"Yup. And we have a shot at the play-offs. You'll enjoy that."

It wasn't an easy choice for me. I was the girl who was never going to let a guy stand between me and what I wanted. What I wanted was to write about sports, and my favorite sport was men's lacrosse. But I knew it was the only fair choice. The guys on the team didn't need clever put-downs or doses of praise. They deserved solid analysis, like the kind I could produce consistently before, well, before I fell in love.

I stayed late after the girls' game, working on an article about it, proving to myself I could still write decently about some team. When I arrived home, dinner dishes were piled in the sink. Mom had gone to class, and Grandpa was watching the Os game in the living room. I microwaved a leftover square of casserole, then joined him.

"No entrance to the ballpark without your ticket," Grandpa said, holding out his hand.

"Before I give you a copy of the paper, I need to tell you what's happened. And I'm not ready yet."

He glanced sideways, his eyes sweeping over me in a quick, parental check to see if anything was catastrophically wrong. "Okay," he replied. "You've been granted a free pass to the press box. Find a seat quickly. Surhoff's on first, and I think this pitcher's losing it."

He was. While I ate my dinner, we watched several innings of wild scoring, then Grandpa suggested we take a walk. He said he hadn't done his miles for the day, which I knew was an excuse. Walking would make talking easier because we didn't have to look at each other.

We strolled up and down the blocks of our neighborhood, and for the third time that day I told my miserable story. But I fudged: I didn't mention Adam, just that I'd become good friends with a few of the guys. I waited for Grandpa to ask me how that was different from being good friends with Marnie, but all he said was, "Sounds like you did the right thing, Jane."

"It hasn't been fun," I replied, kicking at a loose stone.

"I'm sure. Have you said anything to Coach?"

"You think I should?"

I guess Grandpa heard the reluctance in my voice.

"You don't have to tell Grizzly the exact reason you've struggled to keep your objectivity. You don't have to give a name and jersey number."

I glanced up at him, surprised. Had he figured it out?

"Maybe I should get this over with now," I said as we started down our back alley. "Coach will still be up."

Grandpa left me at Mrs. Bean's gate. A minute later our neighbor answered the door, wearing a silk gown with green parrots all over it. When I said I wanted to talk to Coach, she muttered something about no parties on Thursday night but let me go up. I stopped at the door that led to the third floor and knocked.

"Coach?" I called. "It's Jane." I pushed open the door, called again, and walked up the first few steps.

"Sorry to bother you. I know it's kind of late," I began. Then I realized the bathroom door, which lay directly ahead of me, was closed and water was running—shrieking through the pipes, actually. I hesitated.

"Hi, Daisy."

I took another step up. "Stacy! I didn't expect you to be here—I mean, to be here still."

My cousin was sitting at a square table, her feet up on another chair, looking very much at home in the eating area of Coach's living room.

"When Grizzly got back from school, we ordered some pizza," she said. "Want a piece?"

"No thanks."

I saw the box on Coach's microwave. On top of the small fridge were five green soda bottles with red candles stuck in them. They looked like Christmas, and now that the bathroom pipes had quieted some, it sounded like Christmas. I listened a moment longer. "Are you playing carols?"

"Perry Como," she told me.

As long as I can remember, Stacy had this thing for Perry Como, a singer from Grandpa's generation.

"It's the only tape of his that Grizzly owns," she added.

"I can't imagine why."

She smiled and shrugged, the way she always did when I ribbed her about her tapes of old romantic songs. I felt as if I was looking at the cousin I used to know, with her red hair in a ponytail high up on her head, her shoes off, her favorite kind of socks peeking out of her jeans—knit ones printed with rosebuds.

"Grizzly's washing dishes in the tub," she said. "He probably couldn't hear you with the screechy pipes."

I glanced toward the bathroom, then walked over to the table where she sat. "What do you have there?" I asked. "Looks like sports photos."

She held one up, grinning. "This is Grizzly when he played for Loyola College."

"Cool." She moved her feet, and I sat down for a closer look. They were lacrosse pictures, and despite the fact that the players were wearing "hats," as Stacy called them, she could point out Coach in every one.

162

"I'm going to mat some of these for him," Stacy said. "He needs something up here to make it more like home. But it's a challenge to figure out how to hang things with this big, sloped ceiling." Her eyes were bright; she loved this kind of project. "He needs some pictures of Big Mama, maybe a collage. And I was thinking about a mobile—that would hang nicely in this space."

"Did Mama come home?" I asked, glancing around.

"She's sleeping in the bedroom. Go say hello."

I found Big Mama nestled in the blankets of Grizzly's bed. Her front paw and her tail were wrapped up, and she had some fur to grow, but she purred when I petted her and blinked at me with contented eyes. "Get better, old girl," I whispered. "He needs you."

On my way out of the bedroom I knocked on the bathroom door. "Hey, Coach. It's Jane. Big Mama's looking good."

The door opened. Coach was kneeling in front of the tub, bubbles clinging to his arms, a tall stack of multicolored dishes next to him. "Hi, Jane. I was trying to keep the noise down." He saw me eyeing the dishes. "I kind of let them pile up."

I laughed. "Need someone to dry?"

"No thanks."

"Um, I need to talk to you about something. About the article I wrote."

"In that case, come on in," he invited, and handed me a clean towel.

I knelt down next to him and we went to work, him washing, me drying and stacking the dishes on his wicker hamper. I explained to him about the different drafts, pretty much the same way I'd explained it to Grandpa.

When I'd finished, Coach asked, "Could you give me a copy of the first version you wrote, the positive draft? I'd like to read it to the team."

"Uh—well—" I wondered if my interest in Adam would be obvious. I knew I'd devoted at least two paragraphs to his offensive efforts.

"I'll tell you why," Coach said. "The boys were talking a lot about your article at practice today. They really took it to heart."

"Oh, jeez."

"See, it's not only you that's gotten to know and like them. They've come to like and respect you, Jane. You're not just some writer whose opinion they can squawk about—not anymore. What you think and say truly matters to them now."

"I never thought about it that way." I dried a plate till it was polished. *What the heck,* I thought, *Adam's so angry he won't hear any of it anyway.* "Okay, I'll drop off the draft during homeroom tomorrow."

We finished up the dishes and carried them back into the living-room area. I wished Grizzly good luck in Friday's game, then headed home.

As I lay in bed that night, trying not to think about Adam, my mind turned to Stacy. It seemed strange for a bride, two days before her wedding, to be hanging out with a single guy who was not her fiancé. But tonight was Travis's bachelor party—his last fling, as they say. It was only fair for Stacy to have her last fling too, with her rosebud socks, red candles, Perry Como, and a tender-hearted guy named Grizzly.

SEVENTEEN

BEFORE THE GAME against Dulaney on Friday, Vinny hung around me at the office and talked a lot. He seemed as nervous as he was pleased about his new responsibility, his whole face glowing pink. He wanted to know where I'd be sitting at the game. With Angela, I told him, and higher up in the stands than I used to sit.

When the game began, it was weird not having to watch every second of it.

"You know, you don't have to look at me when I talk," Angela said. "You never did before."

"It's nice to act normal."

"Just don't get out of practice," she told me. "You're still a sports reporter."

When halftime came, we were winning 7–5, but the other team had fought back from five goals down. The tide of the game was turning in Dulaney's favor. I watched Vinny buzz around to interview players, wishing I could shout down some questions to him.

Adam was standing on the sidelines, toweling off his head, glancing around as if he was trying to find someone. He went over to speak to Vinny.

Angela leaned closer to me. "Can you read lips?"

"Only curse words," I replied.

Vinny pointed up in the stands. Adam pulled on his helmet, then turned toward us and scanned the rows of spectators. It was hard to tell where he was looking beneath the visor and face mask. Kelly, who was five rows below us, waved at him. He turned back to the field without acknowledging anyone. Of course, jocks usually didn't wave back since they were supposed to act as if their minds were on the game.

The second half began with both teams on hyperdrive. Dulaney won the face-off, but we swiped the ball from them. Pablo and Adam were turning it on. Passes moved quickly around the box, then Adam cut and with a quick fake eluded the guy defending him. He held up his stick, and the pass zipped into his net. He pivoted in the air, ready to fire the ball at the goal.

"Watch out!" I shouted as a second defenseman attacked him full force with a body check.

Adam never saw him coming—he should've, but he didn't. He took it hard in the gut and was thrown back against the ground.

"Oh!" I gasped, feeling as if someone had just punched me in the stomach.

I waited for Adam to scramble to his feet, but he

lay still. I gripped Angela's arm. "He's hurt."

The referee whistled play to a stop, and Grizzly ran out on the field. Adam's teammates crowded around him.

"Breathe, girlfriend," Angela said to me. "Breathe."

My stomach was as tight as a knotted balloon.

"It's probably nothing, Jane," she said. "He probably just got the wind knocked out of him."

A moment later Adam got up and flexed his arms and back. I could read his body language from the stands—the shake of his head at Coach, the set of his shoulders—he was disgusted with himself.

How many times had I watched a player being taken out by a body block? Usually I wondered how it would change the offensive alignment if a sub went in for the guy down on the ground. This time I didn't care about anything except whether Adam had been injured.

Later, when Marnie had finished practice and joined us, I found myself cringing as another player got wiped out. When a third player was about to get cut in half, I closed my eyes, as if it were going to happen to Adam.

Marnie noticed my reaction. "Are you okay?"

"I will be," I said with determination. Once this game was over, once the rehearsal and wedding were over—once I got over him—everything would be all right.

Mom drove me to rehearsal at the church that evening so she could sit with Aunt Susan, who'd asked her to come for moral support. On the ride over she told me what I already suspected: My aunt and uncle had been putting on a good show but were as worried as the rest of us about the future of Stacy and Travis.

The church selected for the wedding was large, with gleaming white woodwork and tall, rounded windows. Our rehearsal was being held the same time as tomorrow's ceremony, 7:30 P.M., and the sky was glowing with shades of pink, orange, and mauve, making the clear, paned windows frames of color. It was a wonder Travis didn't object to the sunset for clashing with Stacy's hair.

When we arrived, Adam was already there, hanging out with the group of older guys who were ushers, talking and laughing. I probably would have been more comfortable chatting sports with the guys, but I stayed with the bridesmaids, who were telling wedding stories.

With eight bridesmaids, eight ushers, two honor attendants, a bratty flower girl, a confused ring bearer, a worried father, an emotional bride, and an uptight groom, the poor minister had a lot to handle that evening. Fortunately Mr. Clarke, who was host of the dinner that would follow, had already given his instructions to Travis; he was probably at the restaurant dishing out more directions, which made him one less headache for us.

Stacy had met with Reverend Koontz earlier and told him how she wanted things; that, of course, didn't match up with how Travis wanted them. I marveled at the details they argued over—who was standing next to whom, the order in which we'd take our places, the angles that we would face, how many pews to keep between us as we walked up the aisle. It would have been easier for the reverend to direct the Rose Bowl Parade.

It didn't take long for the tension between Stacy and Travis to quiet the jokes and giggling of the rest of us. At one angry point I saw Stacy remove a shoe, gripping it hard in her hand, and I thought she was going to hurl it the way she had thrown her ring. I caught her eye. She smiled a little sheepishly, then removed the other shoe and put them carefully on a church bench, rubbing one tired stocking foot over the other.

With the exception of the bratty flower girl, we walked through our parts as if we were walking on eggshells, afraid to ask questions that might start another discussion. When it came time for me to take Adam's arm at the altar steps, he glanced down at my face for a moment.

"Congrats on the win," I whispered.

"It's not a game I'm proud of," he replied.

Later we had to link up again to walk down the long aisle and this time we said nothing, just silently matched our steps.

I thought the tense rehearsal was finally over when everyone had paraded down the aisle and gathered in the back of the church. Then Stacy remembered the unity candle.

"What's that?" Travis asked, sounding annoyed.

"Just a little ceremony. A nice tradition."

"Do we have to do it?"

"We don't have to," Stacy told him. "I want to. It's a beautiful symbol of married love."

He grimaced. "Haven't we got enough beautiful symbols?"

"It's not *tacky*, Travis," she said, her teeth clenched.

"Did I say that?" he replied quickly.

"You implied it."

"All I'm saying is we've got enough going on in this ceremony as is. Our guests will be starving. Besides, I don't want to try to light a candle in front of people," he added. "My hand might shake."

Stacy reached out for his hand then. She held it between hers and rubbed it softly.

"Stacy," he said, suddenly pulling her toward him, "I'm so nervous. I never thought I'd get this panicked about a wedding."

"Everybody gets that way," she replied soothingly, putting her other hand up on his shoulder. "Once it starts, you'll relax. Really."

"I hope so," he said. "I keep going over lists in my head."

She ran a gentle hand across his forehead. "Everything's done, Travis. We can just have fun now. And if we forgot anything, what the heck!" She put both arms around him, smiling. "If something goes differently than we planned, who cares?"

"I do," he said. "We've prepared for this wedding too carefully to make a mistake now."

"It's a celebration, Travis, a party with the people

171

we love. It's silly to worry about mistakes."

She looked up at him sweetly until he met her eyes and smiled back at her. Several of the bridesmaids sighed. Travis bent down to kiss Stacy, and everyone applauded. I clapped too, and I watched her feet.

"Her toes didn't curl."

"What did you say?" Adam asked, bending closer to me.

"They kissed," I said, "but Stacy's toes didn't curl."

"Usually when two people kiss, they do it with their lips."

I ignored the sarcasm. "Our grandfather told us that our grandmother knew he was the right one for her because when they smooched, her toes curled."

"I see. What did *your* toes do when you and your artist guy kissed?"

His question caught me off guard. "Um . . . does it matter?"

"Yes," he said, "as evidence for your genetic theory."

That's not how I wanted it to matter. "Maybe it's not a genetic thing," I told him. "Did Kelly mention her toes after you kissed her?"

"No," he replied, "no, she didn't say a word."

Then we both turned back to the romantic little scene in front of us. I would've done anything to have been in Kelly's shoes the other night and to be in them tomorrow too—anything, of course, but tell him that.

EIGHTEEN

T HE DINNER THAT followed our rehearsal Friday
night was uneventful. It was a sit-down meal in
a private room at a very nice restaurant. I stayed with
my family at our table, and Adam stayed with his.
Twice I met his eyes in the reflection of a gilt-framed
mirror, but it was probably nothing more than
chance. Anyway, that was as much as he and I saw
each other that night. When we left the restaurant, it
was thundering, and everyone scattered quickly.

Saturday, May 1, began gray and wet, but by
midafternoon it had turned into a gorgeous spring
day. The sky had been washed sheer blue, and every
azalea bush was blooming, every garden blossom
seemed to have popped open, like the flowers in a
Disney animation. If Stacy burst into song during the
wedding, bluebirds were sure to land on her hands.

Mom and I spent quality time at a hair salon, sitting side by side beneath our dryer helmets, our

fingers stretched out for paint jobs. We giggled all the way home. Mom's hair had become shorter and very chic. Mine was twisted and piled high, held by a glittering comb at the back of my head.

When Grandpa saw us, he ran his hand through his thin gray hair. "I knew I should've had mine done. You two are going to show me up."

I put on makeup at home, then Grandpa drove me to my aunt and uncle's house, where I was to put on my gown and help out Stacy. The other bridesmaids and the flower girl would dress at home, then join us later.

Grandpa and I were silent during the ten-minute ride. When he pulled into the driveway, he asked, "Are you nervous?"

"Yes. Are you still worried?"

"You know I always worry about my two best girls," he replied.

I ran my perfectly manicured fingers along the dashboard; it looked as if someone else's hand had been attached to my arm. "Thursday night, when I went to see Coach, Stacy was still there."

"I know," Grandpa said. "I continued on my walk around the block and saw her car in front of Mrs. Bean's house. How'd she seem?"

"Like Stacy. Like good old Stacy, dressing the way she used to dress. She was looking at lacrosse pictures, photos from Coach's playing days, trying to decide how to mat them. She was thinking about doing a collage of Big Mama and putting up a mobile."

Grandpa nodded. "Decorating the way she's

always liked to decorate, with whatever she can find around."

"Yeah. Remember all the dolls she made out of soap bottles? And the mobile she made out of pasta shapes? And that monster we created with stuff from your workbench?"

"That I hadn't given you permission to use—yes, I remember," Grandpa said, smiling.

"I keep trying to figure out what I'd do if I were Stacy," I went on. "Grizzly could never buy Stacy the things Travis can. She'd have to give up the huge house and the expensive furniture and maybe her chance to be a stay-at-home mom—I think she wants that more than anything."

Grandpa rested one arm on his open window, listening to me.

"But there's a lot of other stuff she's giving up by marrying Travis. It seems like you always have to give up something," I said.

"Well, sure," Grandpa replied. "Things change when someone special comes into your life. Both sides have to give up things. The one thing you don't give up in a good relationship is *you*—whatever makes you most you."

Like Mom did, I thought.

"It's been my experience," he continued, "that when you're with the right people, you feel more like yourself than ever. There's a happiness, and a feeling of coming alive to yourself and the other person, that's like nothing else."

I remembered the moment when I scored a goal

against Adam, his dazzling grin, our high five, and how I felt crazed, exhausted, crusted over with mud, and wholly, happily like me. I wished I could feel more moments like that. I wished Stacy could.

"I think she should put off the wedding," I said. "I think she should get to know Coach."

"Me too."

"Then say something to her, Grandpa!" I exclaimed. "You can if anyone can."

"Stacy has seen enough of Grizzly to make that choice on her own."

"Talk to her!" I pleaded.

He shook his head.

"Mrs. Bean says the advantage of being old is that you can say whatever you think," I argued.

"And how often do her children and grandchildren visit?" he asked.

"Hardly ever," I admitted.

"Our job is to stand by Stacy whatever happens, whatever choices she makes," he said, resting his hand on mine. "It's what you would want me to do for you."

I sighed and got out of the car, then turned back, leaning in through the window. "Grandpa, when you gave up the job at *Sports Illustrated,* it wasn't really because you missed covering the home teams, was it?"

He didn't answer.

"You came back for Mom and me."

He smiled. "Could there have been two better reasons?"

★ ★ ★

Three limousines took all of us to the wedding. People who were walking by the church stopped and stared as eight nervous bridesmaids, a flower girl in the middle of a tantrum, her mother, myself, and an incredible bride climbed out. The driver and I helped Stacy with her train as we climbed the church steps and entered the foyer.

The ushers were already there, escorting guests up the aisles. The bridesmaids huddled together, giggling and whispering, checking their lipstick in compact mirrors. At the doorway to the church my aunt and uncle greeted late-arriving guests. Stacy suddenly walked away from us to a room just off the foyer. I hesitated, then followed her.

"Are you all right?" I asked. Her eyes looked glassy to me.

"Fine. I'm fine. Keep my parents company, okay?"

"Sure," I said, and left her alone, figuring that's what she wanted. I joined my aunt and uncle at the double doors and peeked inside the main section of the church.

The altar was terraced with flowers, huge sprays of white roses and tall blue spikes of delphinium. I saw my mother and grandfather seated in the second row of the bride's side. Mr. and Mrs. Clarke had arrived and were on their way down the aisle, nodding at guests as they passed. Next to me Aunt Susan was holding tightly to Uncle Jake's hand, waiting to be escorted.

I searched for Marnie and Angela, whom Stacy had invited to the church as a favor to me. I needed to see their encouraging faces. With my curtain of dark hair swept up and back and my long legs shown off by three-inch silk heels, I felt both excited and vulnerable. I wanted Adam to see me like this, and yet I was almost afraid of his gaze. When he looked, what would I see in his eyes?

But it was too late to worry about that. The ushers rolled the white runner down the aisle, the music changed, and the minister, Travis, and Adam walked out in front of the altar. I peered down the long aisle at Adam—*Breathe, girlfriend,* I told myself—then pulled back quickly when I realized the guests had risen and were turning toward the rear of the church. I glimpsed Marnie and Angela, who had slipped into the last row, then hurried back to Stacy.

"You ready?" I asked.

She reached for my hand, but it seemed almost like a reflex action, as if she hadn't really heard me. Uncle Jake joined us.

"Look at my little girl," was all he could say, blinking back tears.

Stacy's friends smiled at her as they lined up. The ushers started down the aisle one by one, then the bridesmaids.

"Stacy, are you going to be okay?" I asked.

She nodded slowly, as if she were dazed. I glanced at Uncle Jake, but he was lost in his own world. I had no idea how to get through to my cousin.

It was my turn to start walking. The flower girl's mother was lining her up between Stacy and me. "Go," the woman urged, waving her hand at me. "Go!"

I took two steps into the church, then glanced back at Stacy. "I love you," I said, surprising both her and myself.

As I walked down the aisle, I kept my eyes on the bridesmaid in front of me. When she veered off to the left as she was supposed to, I looked to my right and saw Adam. He was already staring at me.

He stepped forward, and I shakily took his arm. Then he laid his hand over mine, warm and reassuring. I glanced up at him. He was studying my face so closely, I felt as if I were once again lying in the mud with him leaning over me. I was back at the dance, when his mouth had been just inches from mine and he'd whispered, "Daisy."

Then he let go and we went to our places, leaving a space between us for the bride and groom. The flower girl joined the bridesmaids, and Stacy took the last several steps to the foot of the altar. Her father kissed her, then she slipped her hand in the crook of Travis's arm.

The music stopped, and the minister began. "Dearly beloved, we are gathered here to celebrate . . ."

I'd heard all the words before—Stacy had read them to me several times in the last few weeks. Instead of listening, I thought about Coach, wondering what he was doing tonight. I thought about Angela and Tom, and Marnie's friendship with Josh, and Kelly and Adam. Then all of a sudden, much sooner than I'd expected, we were ready for the vows.

The minister looked up at the congregation and said, "If any man or woman here has reason to object to this marriage, speak now, or forever hold your peace."

I imagined the church doors banging back and Coach, still holding a garden rake, racing down the aisle, shouting, "Don't do it, Stacy. You're mine!"

But he didn't.

I bit my lip, waiting for the inevitable, then heard a quiet voice. "I do."

Adam and I both leaned forward, unsure that we'd heard Stacy speak. She held her bouquet in her right hand and raised her left, like a shy schoolgirl waiting to be called on by the minister.

Travis stared at his bride. The guests murmured.

"You do?" the minister said, blinking.

"He wasn't asking *you*, Stacy," Travis told her.

"Well, I'm answering all the same," she said, and several guests gasped. "I have reason to object."

"Are you out of your mind?" he asked.

"I'm sorry," she replied gently, "but I've finally gotten my own mind back. I can't marry you."

"Stacy, have you lost it? We've planned a perfect life together!"

"*You've* planned it, Travis, and frankly, I've had enough of it—your perfect wedding, your perfect house, your perfect parties, all your perfectly coordinated, boring colors." She held up her bouquet of thirty pure white roses, then hurled it into the congregation.

Arms reached up to catch the flowers, and

someone laughed out loud. It sounded like Travis's great-uncle with the portable TV.

"Go find someone else you can make over into the perfect wife," Stacy continued, "perhaps someone a little more tasteful." She pulled off her engagement ring and placed it in Travis's hand.

"You must be ill!" he exclaimed. "Totally ill." He gazed down at the huge diamond. "You're making a big mistake, Stacy."

"No, Travis. Despite all your worrying, we haven't made one little boo-boo so far. But if we get married, we'll have made a whopper."

"I'm warning you. There's no coming back." His voice shook. "I won't be humiliated like this again."

She turned to me. "Grab my train, will you, Daisy? I'm out of here."

I tossed my flowers to Adam, picked up my cousin's hem, and ran behind her, the two of us sprinting down the aisle past the stunned faces of guests. Stacy pushed straight through both sets of church doors and rushed down the steps two at a time. We reached out wildly for the iron railing and finally collapsed together on the church lawn, holding each other, laughing and crying.

"I can't believe you did that!" I gasped.

"I can't believe I almost didn't!"

We laughed and cried some more, rolling back in the grass, then I dragged her to her feet. "Come on," I said. "People are going to be coming out. Quick, into the limo."

"Which one?" she asked, breathless with laughter, tears still streaming down her face.

"Any one. We've got to get out of here," I told the drivers. They looked dumbstruck. Then one of them ran around to his door and yanked it open.

"Where to, madame?" our driver asked as we climbed into the car.

"Three forty-one Brighton Road," Stacy said, which, of course, was Mrs. Bean's house.

NINETEEN

THE LIMO DRIVER dropped us off, then returned to the church since he had a carload of bridesmaid purses to deliver. I slung my rose-and-tassel purse over my shoulder and followed Stacy up Mrs. Bean's walk, still carrying her train. Halfway to the porch, Stacy paused to look up at the third-floor window. The light was on.

"There's no reason to think Grizzly wants to see me," she said. "He's a caring guy, that's all."

I nodded. "He is that."

"I mean there's no reason to think he feels anything special for me," she explained. "How do I know he even wants to see me?"

"You won't until you ask him," I replied, sounding like Marnie.

Stacy looked toward the street as if she was thinking about turning around and running in the other direction.

"Don't make me carry you *and* this train," I said. She laughed nervously.

"Come on," I said, walking her the rest of the way to the door. "Ring the bell. Go ahead."

Stacy licked her lips, then pressed the little button.

"Gracious!" Mrs. Bean exclaimed when she opened the door. The two of us looked a bit disheveled. Strands of my hair were tumbling down from its comb, and Stacy's veil sat crooked. Both of our dresses had grass stains.

"Trick or treat," I said. "Is Coach home?"

"Yes, yes, come in, girls." Her eyes were wide with curiosity. "Is the wedding over?"

"*Very* over," I replied. "Go, Stacy." I gave her a light push toward the steps.

"Daisy, come with me," she begged. "Please. I used up all my courage in church."

"As far as Coach's door," I agreed, "no farther."

When we got to the foot of the third-floor steps, Stacy tapped on the door as lightly as a moth. I knocked harder, then listened.

"What's that music?" I asked, putting my ear against the wood. "It sounds familiar."

Stacy laid her head against the door. "Perry Como," she replied softly.

Footsteps thumped down the stairs, and we both jumped back.

I don't think I'll ever forget the expression on Coach's face when he opened the door and saw Stacy standing there, looking like a pretty bride doll that had run into trouble at the playground.

"Hi, Grizzly," she said, her voice shaking. "I was just stopping by. Do you mind?"

He glanced at me, bewildered.

"Wedding's off," I told him.

I saw the relief in his face. He didn't speak, just wrapped his arms around her. This time there was no question that his eyes were closed as he held her tight against him. I left before he let go of her.

On my way out of the house I explained to Mrs. Bean what had happened. I knew she was dying of curiosity and hoped that with some of it satisfied, she might leave Stacy and Coach alone. Then I headed home, wondering if Mom and Grandpa had arrived yet, thinking the three of us should keep on our fancy clothes and go out for a victory dinner.

As I crossed the alley, I saw a gorgeous moon rising. The sun was almost down in the west and the moon was coming up, a big silver ball that I wished I could grab and dunk in Mrs. Bean's basket. I swung my purse off my shoulder and tossed it into the air.

"Two!" I said as the purse swished through the net. I caught it again. "And Hardy has the ball," I announced out loud, the way I had when Marnie and I had played as kids. "She passes off." I threw the purse from one hand to the other. "And cuts." I ran around two potholes, which wasn't easy in three-inch heels. "Hardy receives the pass. A little shoulder fake and she catches her man off guard. She pivots. It's a right hook!"

The purse soared through the air, hit the backboard, and dropped neatly in the basket. And then it stuck, the big rose caught on the webbing.

"Now what?" I muttered.

From behind me came a burst of laughter. I spun around quickly. Adam was sitting in our backyard swing, one arm stretched casually over the back of it, my bouquet of flowers next to him. He got up and strode to the gate. "Want me to get it?"

"No," I said, my cheeks growing warm.

He looked me up and down, pressing his lips together as if he was trying to keep back the laughter. I knew I no longer looked like an ad in *Bride* magazine. I was sure he'd heard my play-by-play. I felt ridiculous. My high heels wobbled as I crossed the stony alley and entered the gate he held open for me. "So, all dressed up and nowhere to go?" I remarked dryly.

"I had somewhere to go. Here."

I stopped just inside the gate, wondering exactly why he was here and where Kelly was.

Adam tilted his head. "What?" he asked.

"I didn't say anything."

He laughed lightly. "There's a huge question mark on your face."

I turned away from him.

"Jane, I can sense a question coming from you from fifty yards away." He laid his hand on my arm. "It's a skill I learned when you were covering the team. Self-defense, I guess."

He turned me toward him. "I think I need to drop the defense. I've kept it up too long."

The sudden seriousness in his voice made me look at him.

"More questions," he observed. "Ask them."

I glanced down at my feet and kicked some dirt around with the silk toe of my shoe, like I was Mike Mussina on the mound contemplating my next pitch. "Uh, how are you feeling after yesterday's wipeout? Anything hurt?"

"My pride," he replied with a grimace. "I got what I deserved for putting on a show out there."

"It's not like you to do that," I said.

"Yeah, that's what Coach and everybody else on the team told me. Josh said it was time I get my act together—like immediately."

"What'd he mean? You only got dumped once. One mistake—"

"Jane, you know lacrosse! You must've seen the way I played the first half!"

Yeah, through your eyes, I thought. *Even worse, through the eyes of someone in love with you.*

"I spent the whole first half wondering where you were, if you were even there," he went on. "I saw Vinny, but you weren't next to him. At halftime Vinny pointed you out in the stands. And then I went on the field, showed off, and got walloped."

I laughed with elation and relief, then quickly put my hand over my mouth.

"So much for being a disciplined player," he went on, "a team leader whose mind is always on the game. Stop laughing," he said, pulling my hand away from my mouth, laughing with me. "Coach probably would've killed me if he hadn't been so distracted himself."

It works both ways! I thought happily. *It's not just my writing that's affected by him—his playing is affected by me!*

There was still one question, though. "Where's Kelly?" I asked bluntly.

"I don't know. After the dance I became the jerk I'd always hoped I wouldn't be and took back my invitation to the wedding. I couldn't fake it, and she knew it. Where's Daniel?"

I shrugged. "After the dance I sent him off to find another girl to be his mother."

"Did you?" He laid his hands gently on my shoulders. "The thought of you with him has been driving me crazy all week. I couldn't believe how jealous I was! . . . You look so amazed. Didn't you guess?"

"No."

He took my face in his hands. His eyes shone a soft green, the way they had when we'd danced. "Daisy," he said, "I've fallen for you. I'm in so deep, I don't know what to do.

"I'm sorry about the scene outside the cafeteria. I understand now—Coach showed us the other draft. But when I first read your column, every sentence felt like a knife in me."

I put my arms around him and hugged him tightly, wanting to hug away all the hurt. "I'm sorry. I'd begun to see everything through your eyes, to feel every hit you took as if it were happening to me. It scared me to death to feel so much for you. It scares me still." I could feel the tears rising in me.

He held my face against his. "I love you," he said softly, then moved his mouth close to mine. The touch of his lips was so gentle, the kiss so sweet, I trembled.

"It's okay," he said, "we're going to be okay, you and me."

His arms wrapped around me, and he kissed me again and again. I sighed with contentment, then laid my head against his shoulder.

"Did your toes just curl?" he asked.

"No," I replied, smiling, "but I've always been more like my grandpa, so that doesn't mean anything."

Adam kissed me once more, a long, wonderful kiss, then said, "So what's it mean when mine do?"

o you ever wonder about falling in love? About members of the opposite sex? Do you need a little friendly advice but have no one to turn to? Well, that's where we come in . . . Jenny and Jake. Send us those questions you're dying to ask, and we'll give you the straight scoop on life and love.

DEAR JAKE

Q: *Ben and I are just friends, but the other day when we were getting off the phone, he said "I love you" before we hung up, like it was no big deal. Now I'm so confused! Did he mean something more by that? We've never said it to each other before.*

TM, Guymon, OK

A: A lot of close friends say they love each other without meaning it in a romantic way. However, this usually evolves over time and is a mutual development where both parties know the meaning behind the words. For Ben to suddenly pop out with the phrase is definitely suspicious.

There are a couple of possibilities here. Maybe Ben did mean it in a platonic way, and it just slipped out naturally because he feels you two have grown closer recently and the friendship is reaching a deeper level. Or you could be right that this was Ben's attempt at testing the water and letting you know that his feelings for you go beyond friendship. How do you learn the truth? The next time you talk to him, is he awkward or uncomfortable? Does he seem like he's waiting for some kind of response from you? These would be signs that he dropped the *L* word for a reason. However, if he acts like nothing is different and continues to use more affectionate terms with you than he used to, chances are there's nothing out of the ordinary going on.

Q: *I used to have a huge crush on this guy, Danny, but he wasn't interested in me. Now I'm dating Rob, and I'm very happy with him, but Danny just told me he wants to go out with me. I don't know what to do because I still have feelings for Danny, but I care about Rob a lot too. How do I choose?*

KR, Pulaski, WI

A: Okay, you probably already know this deep down, but here it is: No one but you can make that choice. I don't know who will make you happier or who you are truly meant to be with. All I know is that you have to trust your own instincts. If you stay with Rob, will you be thinking about Danny every second? Is your desire to be with Danny sincere or do you just want to prove that you can finally get him?

What changed Danny's mind? Are you sure that he's serious about this? These are just a few of the questions you need to ask yourself before making such a big decision. Once it's straightened out in your head and you know for sure who and what you want, be honest with both guys so that there won't be any confusion for them or for you.

Q: *I like this guy, Jeff, but he's always hanging out with this gorgeous girl named Vicki who he's friends with. I'm average looking, and I feel like there's no way he would notice me when girls who look like Vicki are around. Do I have a chance with Jeff?*

ML, Oakville, Canada

A: You certainly don't have a chance if you're going to have that attitude. But if you stop ragging on yourself and quit comparing yourself to Vicki, then you might have a shot. Here's something to think about—if Jeff wanted to date Vicki, why wouldn't he? Clearly they're just friends for a reason. When it comes down to it, we want girlfriends who can have a good time and be funny, who are interesting and intelligent, and who know and care about us for who we are. If you think there's a spark between you and Jeff, explore and see where things go *without* using silly excuses to stand in your way.

DEAR JENNY

Q: *My new boyfriend, Paul, has had other girlfriends before, but this is my first relationship. I'm intimidated, and I don't know how to act about it. What do I need to know about this that he probably already learned from his past?*

AD, Jacksonville, FL

A: It's an old story, but it's still true—every relationship is unique, and you can't hold one up to another in any way. Yes, Paul is more accustomed to the position of being committed to someone than you are, but this relationship is as new for him as it is for you because it's totally different from any that he's been in before. You are learning together what makes you both happy and what you are looking for from each other. Don't worry about who has had more experience since Paul obviously doesn't care about that. He chose to be with you, and that's what matters. Focus on getting to know him better, and the rest will come naturally!

Q: *My boyfriend and I come from different backgrounds, and sometimes I wonder if that will be a big problem for us. Can two people who have lived such different lives make a good couple?*

SA, Nappanee, IN

A: I won't gloss over the rough spots here:

It'll be challenging to get past huge differences between you because there will be parts of each other that you'll need to learn to understand. But since you're already in a relationship, I'm sure that you guys are willing to put in the effort. And that's really all it takes, a little time and the ability to listen and be sensitive to each other's experiences. In the end, you'll both benefit from having your perspectives on life broadened.

Q: *I'm frustrated because although my boyfriend says he loves me, he just doesn't act excited when I'm around or when I call him or anything. I want to feel like I make him as happy as he makes me. Am I just being petty?*

AC, Saco, ME

A: It is absolutely not petty of you to want to see signs of affection and appreciation from your boyfriend. However, you weren't too specific about how serious the situation is. Some guys just aren't very bubbly or open about emotions, and so no matter how psyched they are to be with you, they don't show it easily. The solution? Give it the tried-and-true approach—honesty. Tell your boyfriend that you feel hurt by what you perceive as a lack of responsiveness on his part. Reassure him that you're not trying to make him into someone he's not, and you'll understand if it's not in his nature to go crazy the second he picks up the phone and hears your voice. Then explain that all you need is some sign that this relationship means as much to him as it does to you, and you want the two of you to work on ways to keep things clear.

Do you have questions about love? Write to:
Jenny Burgess or Jake Korman
c/o Daniel Weiss Associates
33 West 17th Street
New York, NY 10011

Don't miss any of the books in *Love Stories*
—the romantic series from Bantam Books!

You'll always remember your first love.

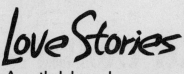

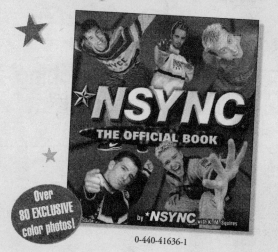